Can *in your* *house*

the pineville heist

LEE CHAMBERS

PUBLISHING

THUNDER BAY, ONTARIO, CANADA

Library and Archives Canada Cataloguing in Publication

Chambers, Lee, 1970-
The Pineville Heist / Lee Chambers

Also issued in electronic format

ISBN # 978-0-9864943-1-4

I. Title.

PS8605.H343P55 2011   C813'.6   C2011-905297-0

Printed in North America.

Edited by Julinda Morrow
Cover Photo: Shutterstock

A #1 BESTSELLING THRILLER ON AMAZON

the pineville heist

"An electrifying debut novel -

Masterfully written and executed, Pineville Heist is a must read. It is the very definition of thrill, energized with edge-of-your-seat action and suspense."

MIHIR SHAH - US REVIEW OF BOOKS

"Fantastic! I found myself turning pages with intrigue. This story commands your attention and doesn't let go."

STRATTON LAWRENCE – CHARLESTON CITY PAPER

"Lee Chambers' debut novel delivers hairpin turns with every page. I loved it! It's impossible to put down."

DANA MICHELI – WRITERS IN THE SKY

"An action-packed thriller filled with plot twists that keep the reader turning pages."

NANCY FAMOLARI – BOOK BLOGGER

"The Pineville Heist is a good actioner for young adults. Chambers has talent and a fine visual sense."

HUBERT O'HEARN – CHRONICLE JOURNAL

"A captivating mystery with action crammed from cover to cover."

BEN WELDON – READER VIEWS

"An enthusiastic five stars!
This is a young adult thriller with a slick plot
at a breakneck pace that will no doubt
appeal to adults as much as to teens."
AMY JONES – THE WALLEYE

"An amazing read for all -
An adrenaline pumping page turner."
AMANDA'S CHICK LIT

"Readers that like fast-paced action will enjoy this
adventure with twists and turns. Teens will love it!"
BEVERLY STOWE MCCLURE – BOOK BLOGGER

"A delightfully thrilling fast-paced mystery
that is action packed from beginning to end."
ISABELLA GALLATIN – BOOK GARDEN REVIEW

"A gripping fast-paced novel that
will keep you on the edge of your seat."
CHRISTINA IRELAN – INTOXICATED BY BOOKS

"If you want a good suspenseful terrifying thriller I would
definitely suggest reading The Pineville Heist."
MICHAEL LICHTENBERGER – THE BOOKSHELF REVIEW

FOLLOW PINEVILLE HEIST MOVIE AND BOOK NEWS AT:
www.pinevilleheist.com

dedication

For Alex and Lesley. My parents.

acknowledgements

While this debut novel is based on my original story and characters, it could not have been written without Todd Gordon, with whom I share the writing credit on the award-winning screenplay, from which this novel is based. Designed as my feature film directorial debut, the process of crafting the book version further cemented my ideas about the characters and allowed me greater freedom to explore much more than the screenplay would permit.

I am also grateful to Julinda Morrow, Tara Dixon, Elle Andra Warner, Toby Osbourne and John Halasz for assisting me in this process of turning this story into a book.

one

AARON LOOKED STERNLY at himself, his reflection staring back at him. His dark hair was wispy, and his handsome, sharp features were accentuated by his smart designer clothing. He straightened up, relaxed his arm, shook his wrist to release the tightness, and then brought the open book in front of his eyes again. He glanced briefly at the page, inhaled a deep breath and then lowered the book to his side, so he could face the floor-length mirror attached to the back of his closet door.

"But to my mind, although I am a native here, and to the manner born, it is a custom. More honored in the… in the… Shit." Aaron crumpled shut his eyes in frustration and sighed, releasing the remaining air from his lungs, deflating in front of the mirror. He raised the book, a copy of Shakespeare's 'Hamlet', and scanned the sea of words for the correct line.

Just as Aaron found his place on the page, he heard the familiar creak of the staircase. His father's weight made that type of creak. Without knocking and much to Aaron's chagrin, Derek Stevens, Aaron's dad, swung open the bedroom door and waltzed inside.

"Didn't you hear the intercom, Aaron?"

Aaron simply glanced at the reflection of his father, without turning away from the mirror. Dressed in a shark-skin suit and a slick black tie, Derek was stone-faced, as usual, with slightly receding hair and deeply-set eyes. Even with the same sharp

9

features and clean cut appearance as his son, the similarities ended there; the fifty-year-old man couldn't remember, or perhaps didn't care to, what it was like to be seventeen. Yet, just like Aaron, Derek's clothes were all designer labels; his hair styled as slick as his wardrobe. And both of them, father and son, looked sullen and utterly unimpressed with the other.

"I'm leaving now. Let's go!" Derek barked, marching out of Aaron's bedroom in a huff. Aaron closed his eyes in frustration and opened them slowly, sharing a knowing look of annoyance with his reflection. Then he turned on his heels and scuffed the shag carpet as he crossed the massive room to his even more massive desk. Picking up a red binder lying next to his top-of-the-line computer system, Aaron dragged himself away, passed the various shiny, pretty objects in a room filled with high-end toys and gadgets, stereo equipment, exercise gear, a big screen TV, and shelves lined with Blu-Ray and Playstation game cases.

From the exterior, it appeared like Aaron had everything a kid could ever want. But, Aaron had learned to be jaded by the materialism of his father's lavish estate, gifts and clothing. Growing up surrounded by luxury tended to make the rest of the world seem shitty and unforgiving. While growing up in Pineville, population 3902 confirmed it.

Aaron hurried down the sweeping marble staircase to the front doors, a massive set of double doors. Made of solid oak inset with elaborate geometric windows, the doors together totaled ten feet high and eight feet across. They lead out to a marble porch, which was decorated with elaborate potted plants, trees really. As Aaron hurried down the slate walkway lined with an impeccably maintained and elaborate bed of bright flowers, he glanced over his shoulder for a glimpse of the colossal mansion he hated, an imposing structure similar to the homes featured in architectural magazines. In the distance, the smokestacks of an old mill loomed over the main street of a quintessential small town.

The town was settled nicely next to rocky cliffs and featured tree lined streets and fresh air; a haven for bringing up a family. Wire flower pots lined with moss and brimming with flowers and vines hung from every other lamp post, and blue banners that featured the upcoming town centennial floated gently in the breeze on the other lamp posts. This quiet place, which was once rich with an industry on the move, was now a simple town with many closed storefronts. Only the basic amenities of a grocery store, a fire station, a bank, a travel agency and several other essential community staples remained.

"Took your sweet time," Derek snipped as Aaron slid into the backseat of an idling limo, its door already open. The limo immediately pulled away from the palatial Stevens residence and rolled down a meandering driveway, through a pair of wrought-iron gates surrounded by perfectly-trimmed, thick, green hedges, and into the outside world.

Derek was busy typing on his smartphone, while Aaron opened his red binder, where he had tucked the well-thumbed Hamlet book. He started mouthing lines to himself, drifting away from the frosty tension in the limo and immersing himself into a completely different reality. "By the way, I can't make it Monday," Derek murmured off the cuff, killing the silence.

Breaking his concentration, Aaron's wide hazel eyes shifted to his father before he slapped the book shut. "Your play," Derek continued, nodding at the book. "I'm going to be tied up all day finalizing the mill situation. Anyway, you'll survive, right?"

"I did for all the others," Aaron replied, nonchalantly. He stared at his father for a moment, feigning the nonchalance he had voiced.

An irritating shrill ringtone permeated the limo as Derek's phone illuminated in his hand. Derek brusquely snapped it open and, while intensely staring into Aaron's eyes in a contest of wills, barked, "This better be good news, Phil."

Aaron turned to look out the tinted window, disappointment brimming in his eyes, cutting a frown on his forehead. He watched as the town began to stream by his window. Suddenly, Derek's comment was followed by a loud crack, as he ploughed his fist into the door panel.

Drawing back his knuckles, Derek looked disapprovingly at the blood that had risen to the surface of his skin. "I've already deposited the five million. What more do they want?" he said, suddenly calmer. "The mill's not worth it, Phil. I'd rather mothball the place than accept that..." Derek paused, noticing that Aaron was watching him out of the corner of his eye. "Look, I'll call you back," he concluded the call abruptly.

"What's that about?" Aaron asked, with a hint of concern in his voice. It wasn't like his father to raise his voice and show anger.

"It's just business." Derek then deftly deflected the conversation as he always did. "Maybe if you took some classes on how the real world works instead of learning how to prance around in leotards, you'd understand a little more about what it is I do."

Aaron rolled his eyes at the typical remark. "You mean sitting in your office pissing off the whole town while you get richer and richer?"

He had a point; pretty much everyone in Pineville worked at the mill, making money for the Stevens family, money truly taken off their own backs. The mill was a processing plant that turned the nearby woods into practical requirements for the home as well as into works of art.

The success of the mill was all thanks to Derek Stevens; he invested in the mill in the mid 80's before the boom and benefited from it greatly. Derek was a savvy investor who went to New York with his inheritance when he was young and made a killing on Wall Street before returning to his family's roots back in Pineville.

In the beginning, Derek was a local hero. He was respected and liked. Admired for his kindness. The town existed because of the mill. For if there was no mill, there was no Pineville. Off the beaten track a bit, Pineville had no other options for growth; no options to sustain itself. Tourism maybe. But, other than being a pretty town, it had no drawing features. The town needed the mill and, for years, it prospered.

Nowadays, however, Pineville was finding it tough as the market of finished wood products was changing. The Chinese were largely to blame. Even though Pineville's products were better, the Chinese hustled in on the market by cutting corners, paying low wages and undercutting on prices. Everyone wanted a deal and suddenly the boom of the 80's and 90's disappeared and customers moved away from Pineville quality to cheap flat-pack, easy to assemble stuff. No one wanted to cough up for quality anymore. Times were getting tough, hard to survive.

The once respected Stevens' name was now a curse. While the mill faltered and bordered on collapse, the man most closely associated with the business, Derek Stevens, still enjoyed his vast wealth. Angry that the recession wasn't affecting the town equally, many of Pineville's residents, and mill workers, were turning on the Stevens family. The town was on the verge of bankruptcy and they needed someone to blame.

For most, the writing was on the wall. As majority stake-holder, rumor had it that Derek was about to make the harsh decision to shut down the mill. The announcement would be a blow. People feared for their future. There were many that were downright mad and outraged that Stevens seemed too interested in protecting his personal wealth.

Recently, the signs were going up. For sale. For rent. Fore-closed. Homes began flooding the market. All at once. Every-one was trying to sell, but no one was about to buy into what may soon become a ghost town. A blip on the map. Thanks for visiting Pineville. Gone.

And Aaron was caught in the middle. The only son of the rich man on the hill. Still seen as part of the cursed Stevens' clan, yet disdainful of his father's actions.

"Hearing you right now it becomes more and more obvious every day how right your mother was," Derek said, shaking his head, returning his attention to the text messages on his smartphone.

"About what?" Aaron asked quickly. Discussions about Sandra Stevens always got the hair on Aaron's neck up. Struck down with breast cancer in her prime, the loss was crushing for 14 year old Aaron. As his Dad was always at the Mill or away on business, Aaron gravitated to his mother. It was Sandra that raised him and encouraged his creative endeavors. Losing her was tough. Now a single parent, Derek was forced to be a father and he wasn't having an easy time.

"How you just don't... get it." The words "get it" hung around in the air like a bad smell. Aaron had heard it all before, of course, but this time it seemed more personal an insult than usual - it was only a matter of time before his emotions would untangle from the knot in his stomach and join the heated conversation.

"Get it? Yeah, well, listening to you lately makes me realize how wrong she was about you!" Aaron said in an explosive outburst, as he pointed his finger precariously close to his Dad's face.

Derek waved his hands. "Stop the car."

two

A pair of eyes unplucked themselves from the road to look into the rearview mirror. "Sir?" the driver enquired, as the limo rolled up on Main Street.

"Stop the goddamn car!" Derek spat, saliva beading in the corners of his mouth.

The driver immediately slowed the limo next to a white van, just as it was about to pull out from the curb. Aaron heard the squeal of the brakes and took it as his warning signal to get ready to be ejected. "You want me to walk from here? It's your fault I'm already late." But, it was pointless. Aaron could see the serious look on Derek's face – daggers protruding from his irises, with the cutthroat vengeance of a businessman who had done his share of dog-eat-dog deals. "Fine!" Aaron shouted as a parting shot, exiting the limo into the cool morning breeze.

The chill in the air was all the more eerie when the man behind the wheel in the white van pounded his fist on the horn, honking in protest at being cut off by the limo. Aaron kept his eyes on the ground, until he heard Derek call out, "Hey!"

Aaron turned back to the limo just as the Hamlet book was contemptuously tossed out of the lowered rear window. It hit him in the chest and fell to the ground, in a shallow puddle that had pooled near the gutter. Aaron cursed under his breath as he squatted to pick it up.

As he straightened and stepped onto the sidewalk, he watched the limo disappearing in a cloud of exhaust smoke. His eyes aimlessly crossed paths with the man in the white van, who was looking directly at him. Although a beard consumed much of his face, above it, the man's beady bloodshot eyes were piercing and fixated on Aaron. He pumped his balled hand at Aaron as the driver pounded on the horn again, letting rip with a blare that almost tore holes in Aaron's eardrums.

Aaron started walking as the bearded man and his partner peeled away in the white van and then he glanced down at the damp squelchy object in his hand. "Oh man!" The book was sodden and dripping. He shook it off as he walked up Main Street, passing outside the town's bank.

With a strip of silver chrome running along the exterior, the bank almost appeared futuristic in comparison to the surrounding stone and brick buildings. However, the Pineville Savings and Loan was still very much in Pineville, evidenced that morning by a handwritten sign, hanging in the bank's window: *Gone To Lunch. Rosie.*

Leaving behind the confines of the overly cheerful Main Street to take a shortcut through the woods, Aaron began to push the limo ride with his father into the recesses of his mind. Here he was, in the forest, his favorite place to get away from everything – the materialism, the expectations, the boredom. Towering, ancient tree trunks surrounded him, along with the sounds of a babbling brook and a few birds, chirping in the branches above. This was Aaron's own private stage where he could rehearse, relax, and forget about his troubles. Nobody would judge him, he could speak his lines as loud as he wanted, and nobody would burst in and boss him around. It was just him and nature.

A twig snapped, and Aaron stopped in his tracks. He looked around to make sure his private oasis wasn't invaded by an intruder. Nothing – then a flash of movement. A rabbit, running from its burrow. Aaron sighed and smiled at himself.

"Here, thou incestuous, murderous, damned Dane!" he called after the fleeing rabbit.

Aaron continued to stroll deeper into the forest; thick brush at his legs made him walk in high steps, while spindly branches near his face made him duck and weave. As it became denser, he pushed the copy of Hamlet inside his red binder, and slotted both into his jacket, zipping it to his neck. The shadows were closing in around Aaron; the sky was now barely visible through the shroud of intermingling tree boughs. He looked up, looking for the sun, only to find the towering pines he knew so well reaching toward the sky. He forged on, looking for the path he had accidentally strayed from.

Breaking off a piece of branch, Aaron emerged onto a muddy pathway, smudged with tire tracks. At the end of a long line of tread marks, the white van was parked, with dirt specks sprayed all across its back doors. Aaron's brow furrowed. "What the hell?" he thought as he tentatively plodded in the direction of the van, each footstep mired in muck.

Slowly, Aaron leaned over to peer inside the driver's side window. There was no sign of the bearded man, just the interior of a well-lived-in van, with a dangling tree air freshener and empty paper coffee cups. Then something caught his eye – beneath the car seat, there appeared to be a pair of gloves and some kind of uniform rolled up, like it was hastily hidden away.

Another crack caught Aaron's ear. Much farther away this time. Probably just the rabbit, hopping along. Probably.

three

Jake in a sweat-stained checkered shirt, filled out by burly shoulders, worked away with a shovel. This was the bearded man. He stopped to catch his breath and then turned to another man just as gruff-looking who was standing over him watching. "Pass it over, Gordie."

The man, Gordie, a clean-shaven 30-something, handed Jake what he wanted – a stuffed green backpack. Jake shoved it into the freshly-dug hole and admired it for a second. It looked tiny and lost inside the large hole.

"Should I put a stick in to flag it, Gordie? He won't be able to find it without a bloody tour guide."

Gordie reached into his jeans' pocket and retrieved a black GPS unit. "That's why he gave me one of these, genius." Gordie recorded the coordinates as he moved deeper into the woods. "Come on - we still need to stash the other backpack and dump the van."

Jake groaned and watched Gordie walking away as he wiped the perspiration from his neck with a handkerchief. "Lazy bastard," he murmured. "Wouldn't take so long if you picked up a shovel."

With a second thought, Jake reached down and unzipped the backpack, carefully, easing through each tooth of the zipper to ensure an almost silent opening. He touched the canvas bag within the backpack – stenciled with the words: PINEVILLE SAVINGS AND LOAN.

"Don't take all day," Gordie called out.

Nervously, Jake retracted his hand and turned his coveting eyes away. Zipping the backpack closed, he proceeded to bury it in a pile of dirt. "Goodbye – for now."

Leaving the hole mostly unfilled, he dragged a wooden board over and placed it on top. Then he kicked some soil and leaves over the plank of wood, disguising it, blending it with the rest of the forest groundcover.

"About time, genius," Gordie coughed as Jake joined him.

"No need to be a jerk," Jake said. Finally he'd had enough.

Gordie turned to face Jake, examining him with his steely unblinking eyes. He recognized he was pushing boundaries. "Okay, Jake. Relax. Stash this second backpack and be quick about it. Unless I've hurt your feelings?"

Jake shook his head. That was good enough, he supposed. "Give it to me." Jake snatched the backpack and ventured off into the woods.

Gordie scanned the trees and breathed a sigh of relief. A smile crept across his face. He called out to Jake. "C'mon! Hurry up."

Soon both men were returning to the white van. "That was just too frigging easy," Jake laughed, suddenly feeling free of the burden of what was safely stowed in the backpacks, deep in the woods.

"Don't count your chickens just yet," said Gordie.

Jake opened the passenger's side door and turned around, holding the gloves, two security uniforms and two Halloween masks, what appeared to be a zombie and a Frankenstein's monster. "Why do you always have to be so serious? Come on, relax. We did it. We're on easy street now, man," Jake said, oblivious to the teenaged-sized footprints in the mud, which he was obliterating with his every step.

four

The Pineville High School was imposing as approached from the expanse of the athletic field. An older three-level brick and mortar monstrosity, the school housed 235 young minds week on week. One of the oldest buildings in Pineville, the school stood strong on the horizon. Built in the late 1800's as part of the railway expansion, the building converted to a school in 1935 when the commuter trains stopped slipping past the town.

Aaron looked up from his mud-caked shoes and picked up the pace. He was really going to be late at this rate.

With a squeak, Aaron entered the polished locker-lined corridors, and didn't pay much attention to the boiler-suited janitor with a mop in his hand, who was aghast that Aaron had left footprints marking his freshly clean floors.

Aaron made a beeline for the nearest classroom on the left – he passed by the walls, covered with famous literary quotations and paper flyers touting various school productions of plays by Steinbeck, Miller, Mamet, and Shakespeare. He knew by the noises inside the room that he was indeed late for English, with Miss Becker.

Miss Amanda Becker. She wasn't like the other teachers. In her mid-20s, in a skirt, heels and a blouse, she was the thing of teenaged fantasies. A teacher in the ballpark age of her students – and in the tight clothes that challenged every boy's mind to focus on Shakespeare. She tossed her straight sandy blonde hair often, and her glossed lips looked angelic as she helped the students speak in 17th century prose.

It wasn't inconceivable that any one of them had a shot with her. It wasn't outside the realm of possibilities. One day their age differences wouldn't matter. So, perhaps, maybe, who knows. It happens all the time; there was a case recently featured on CNN, thought Aaron, before shaking it off. Too weird. His mind wandered back to waiting for the right moment to make his entrance.

"This is Shakespeare guys, not Tennessee Williams," Amanda announced from the side of the room. She was watching two boys dressed in Elizabethan clothing as they acted out the final scene in Hamlet in front of an audience of fellow students. "He wrote the words that way for a reason. Keep going."

One of the boys, Mike, leaned on his sword. The plastic blade bent and he looked down as it was starting to give way under his weight. "Do we get to use real ones on Monday, Miss Becker?"

"Yes, Michael, you get to use the real one during the play, now please continue."

"*Now cracks a noble heart. Good night sweet prince,*" Mike said, jumping back into character, as Amanda stepped towards the stage.

Peering into the room, Aaron knew he couldn't wait any longer; he decided to slip in now, and hopefully Miss Becker wouldn't interrupt the rehearsal just to bite his head off. He sauntered in and slid into the nearest empty seat. "Aaron! What time do you call this?"

Aaron released a long sigh. It was going to be one of those days. He looked over his shoulder at Miss Becker and she was already crooking her finger, beckoning him to the back of the class. Her face was a mask of displeasure and nothing like the fantasy conjured up by his television fantasies.

"I thought you took this role seriously, Aaron," Amanda whispered in hushed tones.

"I do, Miss Becker, I do," Aaron whispered back to her, lifting his copy of Hamlet – considerably worse for wear after its dunk in the puddle. Amanda cast her eyes over the disheveled book and it appeared that her disappointment was gaining momentum.

"If you really want to be a professional on Broadway someday, you need to realize how the simple act of being late can affect the entire production. The play is called Hamlet... and you're Hamlet," she said, poking him in the chest with a ruby-polished nail. "That means this whole thing rests on your shoulders. Understand?"

Aaron looked down at his dirty shoes and then back into Amanda's eyes. "Yeah, but it's not my fault. My dad's in the middle of some stupid deal and couldn't drive..."

"Another part of being a responsible actor is taking your lumps and not passing the buck. Okay?"

"Okay, Miss Becker. I apologize for being late," responded Aaron. "Should I jump in?"

"Yes, Aaron, please join the group. We can't practice 'Hamlet' without Hamlet," Amanda said as she patted Aaron on the shoulder.

Aaron moved to the front of the class, glancing back at Miss Becker, who was staring out the window, arms crossed. Just when Aaron was becoming worried that Amanda was extremely angry with him, she pulled herself away from the window, smiled and focused on the group of teens at the front of the stage, assessing their stances and stage placements.

Aaron also assessed the small group, but with a less Shakespearean focus. The group consisted of about ten students, who played the characters of the last scene. Most of the students were dressed in modern clothing, most of which were cheap knock offs from discount stores. With t-shirts, baggy shorts, and tank tops matching the shaggy modern hairstyles, the group looked more apt for a run on the beach than recite classic lines.

The group surrounded the two main characters of this portion of the scene, Hamlet and Horatio, played by Pete and Mike. The two stood facing one another, ready to act out the final scene.

Mike, who played Horatio, was certainly not a modern day gentleman. He wore baggy skater clothing, and his shaggy dirty blonde hair hung in his eyes. Out of character, every move he made was slow and indecisive, but when immersed in his role, Mike became a quick, decisive leader.

Pete had stepped in as Hamlet in Aaron's absence, and he was a poor replacement. Perhaps to challenge the name given him, Peter George Cornelius III, Pete outfitted himself entirely in black and was poked full of more holes than seemingly possible. Three lip rings, a bull nose ring, two eyebrow barbells above each brow, and one large gauge lobe stretcher in each ear were the more prominent piercings, but he boasted of others in places no one – except maybe his girlfriend – wanted to see.

Pete breathed an audible sigh of relief as Aaron approached to take back the Hamlet role. "Thank God, man. Miss Becker is a slave driver," Pete said as he left the stage, winking exaggeratedly and blowing kisses at Miss Becker as he took his seat next to his equally holey girlfriend, Charlotte.

The class laughed at Pete's antics, and Miss Becker hushed the class. "That's enough class. Let's get down to work. We only have a few days until opening day, and we still haven't gone through the entire dress rehearsal."

Miss Becker turned her attention to Aaron and Mike. "Ready to take it from the top of Hamlet's death encounter?"

Mike nodded and threw himself into the Horatio role before Aaron could respond. *"Never believe it. I am more an antique Roman than a Dane. Here's yet some liquor left."*

Aaron jumped in, saying, *"As thou'rt a man, give me the cup. Let go; by God. I'll have't — "*

"By heaven," Amanda interrupted.

"What?" asked Aaron.

"As thou'rt a man, give me the cup. Let go, by heaven. I'll have't," Amanda corrected.

"Oh. Okay," said Aaron. *"By heaven. I'll have't. Oh good Horatio, what a wounded name, Things standing thus unknown, shall live behind me! If thou didst ever hold me in thy heart, absent thee from…from…from…"*

Aaron began thumbing through his sodden book while the students around him whispered. He tossed his book aside in frustration and plucked Mike's from his hands. Aaron furiously sought the line, and when he found it, he forcefully pointed at the line in the book and yelled "Felicity!"

"Aaron, are you prepared for Monday's opening?" Amanda asked, her brow furrowed in concern. "Pete can always step in as understudy."

Aaron glanced at Pete, who looked as horror-stricken as if he'd been offered up as a sacrifice to the Gods. "No, I know my lines," Aaron said quickly. "I just blanked on 'Felicity'." Aaron paused a moment before continuing. "Will you be there Monday to prompt lines if we get stuck?"

Amanda opened her mouth to answer just as a loud rattling cough erupted from the doorway. Amanda looked to the interruption in relief. Sheriff Jay Tremblay was standing there, filling out the doorframe. Even at 54-years-old, he cast a terrifying silhouette, with his tall looming stature, domed bald head and untamed black moustache draped over his crooked mouth. Having caught Amanda's attention, he adjusted the fit of his hat and checked the holster strap over his Colt 45 pistol.

"Alright, gang, put away your scripts and props and listen up. Sheriff Tremblay has been kind enough to drop by and give us a few words," Amanda said, clapping her hands together.

Aaron and the other cast members quickly took their seats. Amanda nodded her head for Tremblay to proceed.

Tremblay looked around the various boys and girls, as if he were scanning them for criminal records, or even inclinations of criminal activity. He raised his furry, graying eyebrows, like a pair of caterpillars growling at each other as they battle for the coveted position of the bare skin in between the eyes. Then, with another rattling cough, he finally spoke, "Don't take drugs."

A geeky student, complete with black glasses, braces and acne, let out an unfortunate and likely involuntary snort, bringing Tremblay's gaze to him. Feeling the heat of the glare, the student dropped any semblance of a smirk and lowered his head in shame.

"You may think Pineville is some kinda Shangri-La and immune to all the crap that happens down in the big city," Tremblay began to rant, almost spitting at the mere mention of the 'big city.' "But I can assure you that drugs are permeating our community here in Pineville just like disrespect to your mothers is ripping apart the nuclear family."

Aaron rested his chin on his arm as he slumped over his desk, suddenly exhausted by his morning. Yet, he kept his eyes fixated on Tremblay who was moving over to the black-board where he picked up a piece of chalk.

"Pop quiz. What's the biggest threat to you kids today?"

"Reality TV," a foreign student said, causing the whole room to burst into nervous laughter. Tremblay remained silent, with his lips held tightly shut.

"Twitter," a pretty girl murmured, leading to more giggles. Aaron smiled over at her, but she didn't return it.

"Alright, people," Amanda said, crossing her arms.

"My father."

Aaron's words killed the laughter and drove the room into a sudden silence - except for the sound of Tremblay breaking the end of the chalk off on the blackboard.

Mike grinned at Aaron while the other students looked scornfully in Aaron's direction, before turning away from him. Aaron's attempt to win praise from his fellow classmates had failed. Amanda made eye contact with Aaron and frowned. She wasn't impressed either.

"Please continue, Sheriff," Amanda urged.

five

"Ten million have tried it," Tremblay said accusingly as he continued to eyeball the classroom of stony faces. "The majority of users are under the age of twenty." He paused for effect before snapping, "Anyone?"

His word echoed off the walls. "Marijuana," volunteered the pretty girl.

"Masturbation," Aaron joked.

Dead silence. Then suddenly laughter erupted from the desk by the door. It was Steve, a bushy haired seventeen-year-old, with equally bushy sideburns and a soul patch spurting from beneath his thin lips.

"Office," Amanda said sternly, her finger directing Aaron to the door. This immediately erased the smirk from his face and eliminated the short victory celebration of at least making Steve laugh.

Expressing his dismay with a loud hiss-like exhale, Aaron rose from his chair. As he scuffed along the aisle, he stole a glance at Tremblay and regretted it instantly. He found himself on the receiving end of Tremblay's iciest of glares. Not a good idea to be on the wrong side of the law, Aaron thought to himself. And this lawman was as prickly as the points on his Sheriff's badge.

Tremblay didn't miss a step and went on to answer his own question: "I'm talking about a fairly new drug called methamphetamine, also known as speed, crank or ice."

"It's not new. Hitler used it," Steve said with all the condescension he could muster, leading to a few chuckles from

31

students. Aaron shook his clenched fist in a 'jerk off' gesture to Steve, and then hurried out the door, suddenly glad to have Tremblay and Miss Becker in his rear-view. They could talk about drugs and crap all day long. He was outta there and free as a bird.

"You want to go too, Steve?" Amanda said, her voice carrying into the corridor.

"It's true, Miss Becker, the Nazis made it out of fertilizer. The Kamikaze pilots used it too, to stay awake and..." Steve's explanations eventually faded into muffled echoes as Aaron kept walking, smiling like he'd won the trip of a lifetime, instead of a one-way trip to detention. Still, there was time for a detour. Aaron deviated to the right, entering into the boy's bathroom.

Just as Aaron disappeared inside, Officer Carl Smith rounded the corner with a lollipop in his mouth. The white stick dangled dangerously from the corner of the young man's mouth, like a cigarette in a Dirty Harry movie. Nevertheless, with his tousled brown hair and lightly-stubbled chin, while he fancied himself as a Harry, he wasn't quite Dirty enough.

Carl stopped dead and tick-tocked the lollipop stick left and right in his mouth, with the flick of his tongue. He breathed in the pine-fresh scent of the freshly mopped corridors. Brought him back to his glory days. He used to rule this school. And now he ruled the town, as the Sheriff's right-hand man.

After a quick reminisce down memory lane, Carl pulled himself together, tugged the lollipop out of his mouth and strolled towards Miss Becker's classroom. He stood by the door watching for a moment. He found Tremblay in the middle of drawing a crude picture of a skull on the blackboard. With an irritatingly shrill and piercing scratching sound, Tremblay meticulously shaded in the brain area with a nubbin of chalk, then turned to face the kids again.

"This is your brain on meth," Tremblay said matter-of-factly. A muted groan arose from the corpus of students. They'd heard this all before...

Amanda was distracted by a light knock at the door's window – Carl was tapping with the end of his lollipop. She smiled at him, a sparkle dancing across her eyes, which she tried to hide, but failed miserably.

"I thought we were meeting after work?" Amanda whispered through gritted teeth, attempting to smile like a teacher robot, and not a girl talking to a boy. Steve looked over appraisingly at Amanda and Carl. Normally pleasant, there was something brutish about Carl's demeanor.

Carl blankly gazed at Amanda's face for what seemed like ages. For a man usually focused and charming, Carl looked tired and irritable.

Amanda looked deeply into his face the entire time, trying to read his expression. To Steve, she looked like a love struck puppy denied attention.

Carl finally turned his head, ignoring her question, ignoring her imploring gaze. Without a word, or an offer to enter, he pushed the door open wider and stepped inside the class.

Amanda stepped back and tried to hide her emotions from the class. Steve watched as Amanda's face fell, as she wiped what appeared to be a tear from her eye, as she turned away, eyes downcast and saddened.

"Sheriff? Can I speak to you a sec?" Carl announced to the entire room, including a slightly bewildered Amanda. He had his hands on his hips, holding onto his belt, like his dignity required it.

Tremblay gave Carl a "what are you doing here" kind of scowl, then crossed the room, barging past Carl out into the hall. Amanda looked back at Carl, waiting for him to say something to her, anything, but instead he turned on his heels and walked out, closing the door.

Amanda studied the closed door for a moment. Carl didn't need to speak. The back of the door seemed to be saying everything to her. She then turned around to find Steve watching her, blinking after a long stare. Did he also hear what the door had intimated to her?

Defensively, Amanda snapped, "What?"

six

Aaron leaned over the sink, face to face with his reflection in the cracked mirror. "*But to my mind, although I am a native here, and to the manner born, it is a custom. More honored in the... in the... BREACH! In the breach, than the observance.*"

He smiled, fairly pleased with himself. Then he turned on the faucet and splashed refreshing cold water over his cheeks. Aaron took two paper towels from a rusty dispenser, dried his face, then stopped – he could hear two voices, right outside the bathroom. The first one sounded like Tremblay? What was that old bastard doing now?

Aaron opened the door an inch, holding his breath as he eased it, hoping it wouldn't utter a creak and give him away. "So, where are we at right now?" Tremblay asked gruffly.

"It looks like they got away with four, maybe five-million," Carl answered, slightly aroused by the size of the numbers.

Holding his silence, Aaron mouthed the words "holy shit" and closed the door again.

"Holy shit," Tremblay balked, seemingly sharing Aaron's sentiments.

Aaron went back to the mirror, grinning to himself. He didn't want to get caught eavesdropping – especially information that was so incredibly interesting! Maybe five million. Even his Dad would consider that a lot of dough... Wait! It probably was his dough! Aaron couldn't resist listening in, just for a while longer. Carefully, he pushed the door ajar again.

Meanwhile, Carl crunched on his lollipop. "Rosie called it in - as soon as she got back from lunch."

Tremblay nodded soulfully. "Good old Rosie. Any witnesses?"

"Someone saw their van leaving the bank. There's already an A.P.B. out on it, but so far nothing." Aaron stiffened in surprise as he remembered seeing a van, next to the bank. The bearded man! Aaron clapped a hand over his mouth to stifle a gasp and he vanished inside the bathroom, accidentally releasing the spring-loaded door too quickly, causing it to bang ever so lightly.

Tremblay's head flicked around, like a rattlesnake. His hearing was damn acute for an old timer. Lifting his hand, he pressed his palm flat against the bathroom door, ready to push, when suddenly the end-of-class bell rang loudly in the corridors. Tremblay looked disconcertingly at Carl and they both walked away, right before they were up to their necks in spotty, snot-nosed teenagers.

A chorus of slamming lockers harmoniously illuminated the corridor. Mike put his sad excuse for a sword into his locker, with a shrug. Then he closed his locker door with a booming bang, revealing Aaron standing behind it. Grinning, Aaron announced, "You'll never guess what happened!"

"You finally learned your lines?" Mike remarked, sarcastically.

"Someone robbed the bank!"

Steve emerged from behind his locker door, plastered with sexy bikini babe posters. "Get out."

"Seriously. But, we can't talk about it here," Aaron added mysteriously. Aaron turned around and walked away without another word.

"Looks like we are bailing on History," Steve said with a cheeky grin. He exchanged glances with Mike and then the pair followed Aaron down the corridor, past a gaggle of giggling cheerleaders and through the main doors.

The trio burst out onto the side lawn of the high school. The late afternoon sun shone bright and the grass, newly cut, scented the air. Aaron breathed in the freedom and smiled. From the back of the school came the shouts of the football coach and the grunts of the players.

"Crap, we are going to have to sneak past Coach Houston and the team," Aaron realized.

Steve glanced towards the field, looked at Mike and responded, "You up for it?"

Mike shifted his feet. From left to right and right to left; he contemplated their danger for a few minutes before he finally agreed, but with a little less self-assuredness. "Um, yeah. Sure."

Aaron looked around plotting their escape. To the left was the athletic parking lot, and to the right the school. Behind them lay the student parking lot, and the entire athletic field lay directly in front of them.

The football field, in its entire splendor, featured the team and the coach as they pummeled dummy carts. Coach Houston yelled out, "Let's go again, girls!" Half of the team set up and held the dummies while the other half prepared to tackle.

On the coach's feral cry, the players roared and rushed the carts, each tackling the dummies within seconds of each other. Mike, Steve and Aaron listened to the primal grunts and the loud connective 'Wham!' that half of a football team made against a field of dummies.

"Um, guys... I'm not sure about this," said Mike.

"Don't be a wuss!" Steve lamented. "We just have to be quick."

"No, I think we have to be careful," argued Aaron.

"Careful, quick and lucky," Steve chimed in.

"Oh boy," said Mike while biting away on his fingers.

"C'mon guys," Aaron said sternly. "I'm telling you. I saw the robbers. It was them. We gotta do this."

Mike looked worryingly at Steve. Steve stared towards Aaron, then squinted his eyes "What's your plan?"

"Well…" Aaron said while staring towards the field. "We have bleachers to hide us half of the way. But then we have to make a break for it. We'll be out in the open for 25 yards, and then we'll be home free in the woods."

"Let's do it!" yelled Steve, a little too loudly.

At the sound of Steve's yell, the coach glanced in their direction, but just as he was turning to look, a player fell face first on the field. Coach Houston spun on the player instead and screamed through his megaphone, "Get up, Girlie!"

Aaron, Mike and Steve took their chance and ran for the bleachers.

The player, covered in grass stains, pulled himself up and joined the team in jumping jacks. Coach turned to look toward the school, where the boys had stood. No one. Coach shrugged and turned back to the team.

"Oh my God, that was close!" Mike stage whispered to Aaron and Steve. "I was pretty sure we were getting detention for the rest of the year. You better not be screwing with us Aaron."

Aaron, focused on the task at hand, ignored Mike. From their hiding place behind the bleachers, Aaron could see glimpses of the team's workout. The team jogged back and forth across the field, entering and exiting the boy's line of sight while they sat in wait.

"We should probably move to the end of the bleachers to wait for our opportunity," Aaron said quietly.

"OK, let's go," Steve said, a little too loudly again.

The coach perked up at Steve's voice and cocked his head in their direction. The boys stood still, and they held their breaths while the coach tried to hear another sound. Steve shifted his foot and accidentally kicked the bleachers, and the scraping sound seemed to reverberate across the entire field.

Coach Houston looked directly at the bleachers, almost boring a hole into each of their heads. Mike flinched and hissed as loudly as he dared, "He can see us."

"No, he can't," Steve reassured, quietly this time.

The coach stared for what felt like a full minute. Finally, with his team impatiently fidgeting in front of him, waiting for their running orders, Coach Houston turned his attention back on the practice.

The boys breathed an audible, but quiet, collective sigh of relief. They each allowed their loudly beating hearts to settle before deciding to continue. Motioning with one hand for Mike and Steve to follow him, Aaron led the way.

They tracked along the rusty frame of the bleachers, and the two story seating structure managed to contain them for the majority of the field. Reaching the end, they peeked around toward the practicing team where they find Coach Houston staring directly in their direction.

"Get back," hissed Aaron, who was the first of the three to spot the searing stare of the coach. Mike and Steve scrambled back to the comforting security of the bleachers, and Aaron joined them.

"Maybe we should go back," Mike said, pleading in an almost questioning tone.

"Trust me, Mike," Aaron said, looking dead into Mike's eyes. "This will be worth it." Mike curled his lips and gulped, nodding slightly in agreement.

The boys sat for a few minutes, and soon they heard Coach Houston, larger than life, once again bellowing out orders to the team. His barks and jeers echoed around the stadium. Aaron peeked around the bleachers again, and relaxed his shoulders when he saw Coach Houston as he monitored the sea of athletes in a sweaty synchronized set of sit-ups.

"We're good to go," Aaron said, waving Mike and Steve to the fence, which was slightly downhill from the field.

The three walked alongside the fence, and as they ventured around to the far end of the track and away from the action on the field, they felt almost carefree. Almost.

When they reached the end of the hill, they dropped to an army crawl and elbowed their way up the hill to stare at the practicing team. The coach was still yelling commands into his megaphone, and the team was busy practicing their huge, lolling skips -- the exercise that always cracked Steve up.

As the team skipped like little girls across the field, Steve threw his hand across his mouth to stifle a laugh, snorting to hold back his crazy hyena-type laugh. But the harder and harder he tried not to laugh, the louder and louder his snorts became.

Mike looked at Steve in dismay, but Aaron started to laugh as well, although his laugh was a silent pantomime. "They look like fools!" he whispered in glee.

Looking at both of his friends, Mike shook his head and turned away. The coach was looking away now, so Mike said, "If you guys can control yourselves, we can finally get out of here."

Instantly, Steve and Aaron sobered and looking in the coach's direction. His back was still turned, so all three looked at each other and nodded. Then they broke across the field, under the goal post and past a smaller set of bleachers, without being spotted by anyone.

They dived into the woods and ran for a few yards before high-fiving their victory.

Aaron glanced over his shoulder, like a spy in some pulp novel. They weren't noticed.

Seven

Steve and Mike were already moving ahead and began talking excitedly – and loudly – about spending the bank robbery money as they walked deeper and deeper into the woods. "First thing I'd do is buy a Porsche. A black one," Steve chirped.

"Boxster, Nine-Eleven or Cayman?" asked Mike, as if this was a realistic possibility.

"Nine-Eleven. Duh."

"Carrera, Targa, Turbo or…"

"What are you guys talking about?" Aaron chimed in.

"The money. If we find it," Steve nodded.

"Yeah, what are you going to do with your share?" Mike poked Aaron in the ribs; playful roughhousing.

"He doesn't need it, dink, he's already loaded."

"We're not keeping it," Aaron said authoritatively. End of story.

Steve and Mike halted in their tracks. "What?"

"You heard me."

"Why?" Steve and Mike both said, almost in unison.

Aaron kept walking before Steve and Mike caught up with him. They entered into a denser thicket of the woods, as Aaron finally answered them. "Because it belongs to my Dad, that's why."

"Oh my God, you're kidding, right?"

"What do you mean?" Aaron asked Steve, as he stepped cautiously on the slippery wet stones, crossing the river.

With a single push, Steve toppled Aaron from his footing, and Aaron was forced to step with a splash into the shallow water. "Hey, watch it, these are new shoes!"

"Yeah, bought with the gazillions your old man already has. He's not going to miss a lousy five!" Steve barbed.

"It's not just his, dumbass," Aaron shouted, shaking off his leg as he walked onto the river bank. "The money belongs to Pineville."

"Listen to Mister Morality all of a sudden, sheesh."

"He does have a point, Steve," Mike said, creasing up his forehead with concern. Steve had a tendency to push it too far. All over a bag of imaginary money. Not worth shoving your mates into the water and picking holes in their family. Mike glanced over at Aaron with an apologetic nod. Then, moments later, Steve shoved Mike into the tall grass. "Hey!"

Mike picked himself up and huffed angrily. Then he ran to catch up with Aaron, leaving Steve to trail behind.

Looking into the distance, Aaron and Mike trudged along an old railroad bed, between a set of train tracks. Moss and grass had partially hidden the rails of the rusty old relic, and the wooden ties were rotting beneath the forest floor.

Steve was still fooling around as he balanced himself on the rail. "You idiots ever hear of insurance?" Steve said, concentrating as if he was walking on a high wire between two skyscrapers. "The bank will cover every dollar of that money. Nobody's going to lose out. Trust me."

"And what does everybody do in the meantime, huh?" Aaron retorted. "People need money to survive. They have to get paid."

"Who gives a shit, Aaron?"

"Your father would."

"How do you know?" Steve accused, suddenly breaking his concentration and stepping down from the rail. The game was over.

"He works at the mill, right?" Aaron looked at Steve, already knowing the answer. "Where do you think the payroll is before they cash their checks?"

Steve glanced down at the ground, moodily, like he'd fallen off an actual high wire. "You sure know how to ruin something before it even starts."

The brooding trio walked between the tracks in a quiet frustrated huddle, before Mike said, with an uplifting tone, "Maybe there'll be a reward?" Nobody answered him, so Mike rammed his fists into his pockets and continued on in a collective silence.

They left the railway tracks and walked onto a path into the woods, where Aaron had seen the van. "It was parked right here," Aaron said, pointing to an empty void.

"Sure it was," Steve rubbed his chin and rolled his eyes.

"I'm not lying." Aaron saw that the tire treads and footprints had all merged into a quagmire of sludgy mud, each print indiscernible from the other.

"You believe him, Mike?"

"I... I don't know," Mike stuttered.

"Screw you guys." Aaron raised his middle finger and then stomped off down the path. The van was gone and so was any shred of his story's credibility.

eight

"Come on, Aaron! I'm kidding," Steve said, trying to catch up. The thrill of the chase amused him, until he struggled to uncurl his lips and look apologetic. Aaron turned just in time to see the remnants of Steve's stupid grin.

Mike was looking down at his feet, pensively. "What do you think happened to it?" he pondered. His quiet and detached tone was disarming; caused both Steve and Aaron to glance over and consider his question carefully.

Aaron started, "Carl probably found the van right after he…"

"Banged Miss Becker," Steve spat out, finishing Aaron's sentence.

"What?" Aaron asked, snapping his neck to glare at Steve.

"Ewww…" Mike groaned, shuddering at the thought of two authority figures bumping uglies.

"Bullshit," Aaron shook his head.

"It's true."

Aaron walked away again, reiterating his point of view: "Bull. Shit."

Steve shrugged reflectively. "Don't believe me then." He veered off into the woods, muttering as he stumbled through the brush. "It's not my fault your girlfriend would rather do Carl than you."

Suddenly, Aaron was behind him, shoving Steve over. The force of the two palms slammed against his back launched Steve forward, almost tripping over a dead branch.

"She's not my girlfriend, asswipe!" Aaron barked at Steve who had whirled around, wide-eyed.

A flash of anger stole across Steve's eyes as he lunged at Aaron, returning the push, flipping Aaron onto a bush. "Come on, guys," Mike called out, waving his arms like a ref at a boxing match. Aaron bit his lip, before swinging his leg deftly to knock Steve's legs out from under him. With a thud, Steve hit the ground hard; his head bouncing off a small piece of rock.

A guttural roar erupted from deep inside of Steve's chest. He rolled onto his side and grabbed Aaron by the shirt, yanking his face in the direction of his balled fist. "You sonovabitch!"

Aaron felt a searing pain in his jaw, as he lashed out at Steve's eye with the sweep of his knuckles. "She's not worth it, guys!" Mike hollered over their heads, watching the blurring flurry of jabs and slaps.

The fight began to gain momentum and the pair rolled over, so that Aaron had the upper hand. He rubbed his sore chin, eyed his chaffed knuckles, then turned to Steve who was shaking off a dazed expression. "Stop it!" Mike implored, screeching like a girl.

Aaron and Steve suddenly smirked at Mike's over-the-top cry, before laughing at their own ridiculousness, rolling around in the mud, like a couple of kids who'd realized they were arguing over marbles. "Calm down, Mike. And give us a hand, will ya?" Steve said, raising his hand for a lift.

Grabbing their outstretched hands, Mike pulled Aaron and Steve half-way to their feet. The loose dirt was crumbling beneath the sole of Mike's sneaker and then, without warning, he found himself veering downwards – all three now tumbled over, sliding down a steep slope of long grass and slick mud.

A haze of green blades whipping passed their faces. The murky palette merged with the shadows as the boys crashed through the brush at the end of the slope. Their collective yells broke the silence of a small clearing, an old campsite, which they entered en masse, with flailing limbs and mud-smeared clothes.

Aaron leapt to his feet in a cat-like reflex, checking himself for cuts and bruises. The right knee of his designer jeans were torn on a branch on the way down. "Just perfect." Yet, then Aaron quickly thought to himself that the rip had actually improved the look of the jeans ten-fold. He smiled inwardly, as Mike got up and walked to a fire pit in the center of the clearing, full of sooty grey ash.

Mike turned in a circle getting his bearings. Tall pine trees towered over the clearing, and little sunlight peeked through. In the sparse light, Mike could see a derelict lean-to with a shanty-style corrugated roof and an old upturned canoe scattered to the left of the otherwise empty clearing. The ground was littered with brown and red leaves, dried to crisp fall perfection. The leaves crunched underfoot, and a breeze sent a few flying in a beautiful fall dance of life and death. "What is this place?" Mike asked, finding his voice again.

"Looks like a hunting camp," Steve groaned as he lifted himself using a broken branch, dusting his jeans with his other hand.

"In Pineville?" Mike frowned.

"Or maybe one of those old hobo camps when the trains were running," Steve suggested, pointing back up the embankment to the train tracks.

"Hobos had canoes?"

"They could have portaged," Steve quipped.

Aaron laughed. "Portage? Where do you come up with that shit, Steve?"

Steve and Mike made a beeline for the canoe, as Aaron picked up a long stick, ideal for roasting marshmallows on a cold starry night, and he started poking around in the ashes. From absentminded jabbing, Aaron's mind trailed away and he drew a couple of matchstick men in the gray muck. He mumbled, partly as the words formed in his head, "I heard those guys yelling from over here when I saw the van… This must have been their hideout."

"Do you think we can portage this all the way back, Steve?" Mike and Steve weren't listening. Too busy examining the discarded canoe shell.

"How about I portage your face?" Steve said, punching Mike in the arm.

Suddenly, Aaron's stick caught on something beneath the ash – he raised it out of the dust. A pair of wire-framed glasses. "Hey guys…" Mike turned around, followed by Steve, to see the mangled glasses dangling from the end of the stick. "Looks like they burned a body here."

Mike looked horrified and was immediately on edge. "Seriously?!"

"There are some pieces of rags… or clothes, too." Aaron continued to shake the stick through the fire pit, unearthing burnt pieces of clothing.

Steve elbowed Mike in the ribs. "Jeez, you're gullible. It's just a bunch of junk thrown onto a fire by a hobo," Steve scoffed.

A crack of a gunshot obliterated their jovial mood. Steve's face dropped in an instant. Mike froze. Aaron dropped the stick back into the ashes. There was an echo around the clearing as the shot continued to ring out for a couple of seconds – it was from somewhere close.

"They're back!" Aaron hissed in a stage whisper.

Another gunshot, closer than before, succeeded by a crippling scream of pain. A man. Crying out in agony.

"Oh my God, oh my God, oh my God..." Mike broke into hysterics. He and Steve scrambled to the edge of the clearing, quickly looking for cover.

"Come on, Aaron. Let's go," Steve barked at Aaron who seemed paralyzed, standing by the fire pit, listening for the next sound. An angry man's yell. Aaron snapped out of it, just as Steve and Mike ducked behind the bushes near the canoe.

Twigs were snapping under foot – someone or something was heading straight for the campsite. Aaron looked in all directions. Where was the noise coming from? Go the wrong way and run right into the thing making the noise. Aaron spun in a complete circle, his ears trying to penetrate the woods and differentiate from all the crunching and echoes.

Setting a course in his mind, Aaron decided to run to the far left; he crossed the clearing at a gallop, his heart racing – no, wrong move. The noise was getting louder. Someone was plowing through the brush, just a few steps away!

Aaron stopped short, and made a last ditch attempt to hide. Only one place. The canoe. He bolted for it and threw himself across the ground in a perfect slide for home plate. *Safe*.

The "someone" finally arrived in the clearing, just visible from Aaron's vantage point beneath the upside down canoe. It was the bearded man – Jake. He stumbled out of the brush, breathing heavily, and staggered toward the canoe.

Aaron almost let out an involuntary yelp, yet managed to stifle it. Jake's boots were now stomping over, within kicking distance of Aaron's face. After a sharp intake of breath, Aaron clamped his lips closed. Had to hold it shut. Don't make a sound.

Jake slumped over, using the canoe as a crutch, almost tipping it over. Oh God. Aaron squeezed his eyes tight, waiting to be uncovered and discovered. But, the canoe held steady. He almost sighed in relief, but daren't move a muscle. Not till these guys were long gone.

Then another burst of noise. Another someone had bounded from the bushes – so fast, Aaron didn't catch a glimpse of the figure, except for the steel gun brandished in his hand.

"Hold it right there!" a strong masculine voice called out. The sound echoed around inside the canoe. Muffled, but clear enough to Aaron that trouble had arrived.

"You... you don't have to do this," Jake begged, in between labored breaths for air.

"Shut up," the voice said, abruptly.

The fancy alligator skin cowboy boots of the figure stepped closer to the canoe, not far from Jake's cheap imitation leather boots. Aaron angled his neck slightly to see the figure's face, but wasn't about to press his luck.

Jake tried to plead his case. "We got in and out and nobody saw us. Why are you doing this?"

"I said shut up!"

Aaron risked a breath – a silent gasp – as Jake began to sniffle, loudly. Then, the gun cocked with a click.

"Stop crying."

"It hurts, man. It frigging hurts," Jake whimpered. A drip landed on the dirt, a few inches from Aaron's face. And again. And again. Blood. Dark ruby red blood, pooling on the ground.

"Where's the money? And the gun?" the voice interrogated in a harsh and harried tone.

"Please don't kill me..."

"Have it your way."

"Gordie has it!" Jake suddenly cried. No time to be loyal now. Last chance to save your skin. Flip on your friends. Your mother. Anyone to buy a few more seconds of life.

"That's funny, because Gordie said you had both back-packs," the voice said with a playful sing-song to it, like a cat toying with a canary, right before he eats it.

"Gordie's lying."

A strange crinkling sound cut through the thickening tension in the clearing. What the hell was that? Aaron cocked his head, curiosity getting the better of him. His eyes traveled up the figure's scaly boots, to the trouser legs, but that was all he could see; the canoe curbed his line of sight at the figure's waist.

"I think you are the one who's lying, amigo," said the cold voice, sending Jake into a wailing fit of sobs and blubbers.

"Please, no, wait. Ask him again."

"I wish I could, but he's..." BLAM!

Aaron almost jumped out of his skin. The shudder of fast-moving air around the muzzle sent a shockwave, before the sound ever hit Aaron's ears. That was when he knew that Jake was dead. Yet, his ears were ringing so loudly, everything seemed like it was vibrating. He hoped that he hadn't let out a scream when it happened. If he had, he never would've heard it. He didn't even hear Jake's body hit the ground – Jake simply fell into view, pale and flaccid; his cheek slamming against the ground right outside the canoe – mere inches from Aaron's terrified face.

Struggling to control the roll of his dying eyes, Jake looked up and made contact with Aaron. Jake's eyebrows rose, perhaps involuntarily, or maybe in surprise at seeing Aaron beneath the canoe. A wave of blood washed over Jake's brow and down his nose.

Aaron shook his head, trembling, as Jake stared now un-blinking at him. Aaron raised a shaky finger to his lips – *shhh, for God's sake, shhh.*

Jake's tongue fought back against the blood in his throat. He gurgled, "Help me... he's a..." A second bullet was fired, silencing Jake, snuffing out his last words. The flash of the gunfire illuminated Aaron, as he cringed, wishing this nightmare would end and he could just wake-up in his bed at the mansion. *Just get me out of here.*

The alligator boots crunched closer to the canoe, as the figure squatted down, checking Jake's pulse. Then came a husky whisper that sent a shiver down Aaron's spine: "It better be around here somewhere, that's all I can say."

The tightness in Aaron's chest began to uncoil as the alligator boots stepped away from the canoe. The figure shuffled over to the fire pit. He picked up the stick, the same stick Aaron used to poke the ashes and, devil-may-care, started swishing the grass at the edge of the clearing.

Aaron's heart, already pounding faster than he ever thought possible, began pounding even louder, echoing in his ears. The man was not leaving anytime soon, and the longer Aaron stayed beneath the canoe, the more likely it was that he would be found.

Boom, boom. Boom, boom. His heart pounded and drowned out all possibility of reasonable thought. Then his leg started itching, maddeningly in tune with his beating heart. Boom, boom, itch. Boom, boom itch.

Aaron moved his leg slightly, trying to satisfy the itch by rubbing his leg against the ground. Something in his pant leg snagged at his skin instead. A leaf? A bug? Something had slipped in as he slid baseball-style under the canoe. And whatever it was now had the perfect position to tickle him and make him itch.

Boom, boom, tickle, itch. Boom, boom, tickle, itch. As his heartbeat got louder, the tickle became worse and the itch

54

became unbearable. Aaron reached down to itch carefully, and he bumped the canoe with an almost imperceptible knock.

In that exact same instant, in a moment of madness, Steve and Mike made a run for it. They rushed out of their hiding place in the bushes, while the figure's back was turned on them, darting across the campsite.

Their footsteps weren't dainty or quiet. A couple of knuckleheads trampling like a herd of crazed buffalo. They might as well have screamed, "RUN!", because the figure spun around, dropping the stick to the ground once more, and barreled after them, gun raised.

Steve and Mike hurdled the canoe with ease, but Aaron panicked, curling into a ball as the figure jumped the canoe, his foot catching on the lip. In a second, the canoe flipped right over, totally exposing Aaron in his fetal position.

Then another few seconds passed. A gunshot in the distance. Aaron opened his eyes. Nobody. They were all gone.

Aaron unfurled himself and slowly found the will to stand up. At his feet, Jake had bled out. Something then caught Aaron's eye, right out of the corner of his peripheral vision. Stuffed under the seat of the canoe. A green backpack.

nine

Aaron whipped through the long grass as fast as his legs would carry him. His eyes were filled with angst and adrenaline. He was still in shock. Not every day you see a dead man. Not every day you see that much money either – he glanced down at the backpack in his arms. Must – keep – running.

The deeper into the woods that he ran, the thicker the grass and trees got. Branches were lashing at Aaron's face and clothes. The tear in his jeans was just wide enough to allow random thistles and vines to make grazes and cuts on his already scraped knee.

Aaron was nearing the edge of the dense forest. Not much further now. He slowed down, beside a huge uprooted tree, throwing down the backpack, breathless. Looking ahead, there was the clearing leading to the stream, a direct route to the school. Almost home free. He hoped that Steve and Mike were far away from here. They'd all laugh about this later. Suddenly, a branch snapped. He wasn't out of the woods yet.

Aaron threw himself over the uprooted, felled tree and crouched behind the trunk. Suddenly, Aaron remembered the backpack, just out of reach. He periscoped his head to look over the top of the tree, but there was another loud crunch, somewhere in the impenetrable green-darkness of the forest. He ducked and cursed himself.

Another twig cracked into two pieces, beneath the force of the alligator skin boot. The figure's right foot, almost touching the discarded backpack, as it blended evenly with the green foliage.

"I know you're out here..." The figure pulled back the hammer with a telling click. Aaron squirmed uneasily and tried to push himself closer to the tree. Perhaps he could disappear into a hollowed out section, he thought. But, instead, there was nowhere to go. He was cornered.

"It's only a matter of -- aha!" the figure announced, finally finding his prey. Aaron felt a sickening tug in his stomach, like a rope had been attached to his intestines and pulled out through his mouth. With dismay, he rolled away from the tree. It was futile. He was spotted. Game Over.

BANG!

Aaron jolted, before realizing the bullet was not meant for him. Two times lucky.

"Come here, you little bastard..." the callous-voiced figure said, closing in on his target.

Carefully looking over the rotten log, Aaron gazed out into the clearing to see Steve, running across the field, looking over his shoulder. The figure pulled the trigger again.

Another gunshot rang out. Steve spun off balance and collapsed into the thick grass.

"Oh Jesus," Aaron muttered in a state of shock. He turned on his heels, scooping up the backpack and took off in the opposite direction. Not looking back once. He kept replaying the moment in his mind's eye. The blast from the gun. Steve fell down. He didn't get up.

Over and over. Every time the same. Aaron was on autopilot as he splashed across the river, over a select set of stones, then clambered up the slippery slope, back to the train tracks.

Then, a far off gunshot. Aaron dropped the backpack onto one of the rails. Was he hearing things? His eardrums were still jangling from the fatal shot that killed the bearded man. No, it was real. Aaron winced, grabbed the backpack, and raced down the tracks.

By the time that he reached the school fields, Aaron was running out of steam. The backpack was heavier now. Its contents, and the burden of the bag itself, weighing down on him. He crossed the now empty field, lugging the backpack on his weary shoulders, with the Pineville High School tantalizingly close.

Only one car and a van left in the parking lot. Class was out for the day. Aaron glanced at the side of the van, his eyes stinging with sweat and tears. "Chuck's Environmental Cleaning Services: If You Got A Mess. I'll Clean It Up."

Aaron reached the door and found it locked, with a notice taped over it. "DANGER: Asbestos Removal In Progress."

With a desperate fist, he pounded on the doors. Blow after blow. No answer. He lowered his head. Defeated.

ten

Her eyes were one of her cutest features. She checked them out in the mirror and added a sweep of light brown to her left lid. Then, putting down the make-up brush, she closed the compact with a snap – just in time to catch a glimpse of something. A streak of color. Aaron sailing passed the wire-mesh-screened windows. Sweating and agitated.

Amanda frowned. Huh. Glanced at her watch.

"Come on, come on," Aaron gasped, as he raced around the corner and found himself confronted by the door to the side entrance. Open! He yanked the handle and felt the cool breeze of the shady building – all too welcome after running for so long. But, it was no time to take a break. He had to find someone. Anyone.

The metal detectors sounded his arrival with a shrill 'beep' as he continued down the hall with the backpack. Aaron was breathless now, his voice low and raspy. "Help... someone... shot..."

Every footstep was heavier than the last. The polished floors, which were so easily soiled by his muddy shoes before, suddenly seemed to have the upper hand over Aaron. They squeaked in triumph as he struggled to lift his weary legs. Their slippery surface even impeded his traction to the point that Aaron just wanted to keel over, press his face against the cold tiles, and succumb to sleep, numbness, exhaustion...

Yet, the throbbing pain emanating behind his eyeballs wouldn't let him quit. The shrieking muscles in his legs wouldn't let him quit. And most of all, the image of Steve falling down wouldn't let him quit. Just one person, he had to find a single soul, whom he could pass the baton to. Let them run with it. Get help. Save the day. Where the hell was everyone? His sense of time had evaporated. End of the school day he quickly remembered. Classes over, but with cars in the lot someone must still be here.

Aaron arrived at the library. A collection of tools and materials were piled near the heavy wood double doors: rolls of plastic sheeting, a crowbar, scrubbing pads, hand tools, a water tank with a hose attached, and a portable folding-sign - *"DANGER: Asbestos Dust. Do Not Enter"*.

Thinking quickly about the cargo on his back, Aaron tucked the backpack behind the rolls of plastic sheeting, carefully stowing it out of sight. It wasn't a canoe, but it would have to do. For starters, it was bloody heavy. And for seconds, it wasn't the right time to explain what he was doing with all this money. His prime concern was the safety of his friends.

Aaron nodded, inhaled another deep breath, and scrambled down the hall. "Is anybody here?"

Aaron stepped into the reception area of the principal's office. The secretary's nameplate read "Penelope Whittaker," but Penelope was nowhere to be found. Neither was the Principal. Aaron swiftly zipped out of the office and continued down the hall.

Inside the strictly organized and deathly dull confines of Principal Parker's office, the shrouded echoes of Aaron's heavy footsteps were unheard.

Dan Parker, a sixty-something with less than sixty strands of hair perfectly combed across the top of his chrome-domed head (a poor attempt at looking closer to a fifty-year-old loser with a comb-over), was presently pondering Chuck and the stitched name-tag on Chuck's overalls, which clarified beyond a shadow of a doubt that this was indeed 'Chuck.'

Dan wheezed as he lifted himself out of his leather chair, strolled past his family portrait of his wife and 2.5 kids, and ushered Chuck out of his office into a smaller outer office with a desk, chair and an old-fashioned switchboard.

"You promised this would be completed over the weekend, Chuck. The students need to study for exams, plus we have the play on Monday."

At half Dan's age, Chuck was more interested in gleaning a final glimpse of the hallowed Principal's Office. Brought back happy memories of his school days. He never minded being sent to the Principal's Office. More attention than he'd ever received from his own father.

Chuck cleared his throat, probably early signs of too much asbestos dust in the lungs. "You're already red-flagged by the city," Chuck said, pointing upwards at the ceiling. "If I find any of it outside the library, the big boys from the Capital will take over and shut you down completely until it's dealt with."

"Ballpark?"

"Three, maybe four…"

"Days? That's not so bad."

"Months."

"What?" Dan choked. "You can't be serious. Pineville can't survive having the school go down."

Chuck glanced nonchalantly at his hands, dusty and rough. "If what I hear is true about the mill, Pineville's going down the crapper anyway and..."

"Where did you hear that?" asked Dan, feeling a headache coming on.

Meanwhile, Aaron continued, like a ghost flitting through the empty corridors, casting a reflection of a harried teenager in the windows of the closed classroom doors. "Help. Please…"

At this point, he wasn't even sure if he was speaking the words or just willing them out of his mouth, as mumbled whispers and grunts.

Skidding to a halt, relief swept over his aching body. His heart almost exploding as it beat so hard, his head was starting to hurt so badly, from the pounding in his eardrums. The English classroom. The door was open. Amanda was inside. She stood from her desk, putting her cell phone into her purse.

In an insane flurry, a tornado of tension and craziness, Aaron burst into the room. Amanda almost jumped out of her skin. "We have to call the cops!" Aaron screamed out, simultaneously deflating into a heap, collapsed against her desk.

Amanda's eyes quickly scanned Aaron – a horrified glint in his eyes, mud smeared on his ripped clothes, and scratches across his face.

"I think they killed Steve!" he yelled for an encore.

Amanda dropped her purse - stuff spilling out onto the floor. Aaron groaned as he involuntarily bent over, scooping up a lipstick case, an envelope, and phone, handing them back to her. She was now visibly shaking. "Who did? What's going on, Aaron? You're scaring me."

"We have to do something!" Aaron urged, suddenly feeling woozy again.

"Come on," Amanda took him by the arm.

Their footsteps pattered along the corridor, towards the voices of Dan Parker and Chuck, who were surveying the outside of the library. "Well, everything depends on how much crap I find up there once I get going. I tend to find that once I start ripping apart these old buggers, it kind of spreads like a bad case of rectal cancer, know what I mean?"

Dan's face paled, partly nauseated by Chuck's choice of simile, and partly because he knew exactly what he meant. "Just get it done…"

"Mister Parker!"

Dan turned, raising a puzzled eyebrow. Seeing Amanda holding Aaron's arm, he was nonplussed. "What did he do now?"

"I need to call Carl," Amanda said, deadly serious.

Dan faltered in his assurance, with his normally confident and stoic expression falling to one of nervous anticipation. This was not a case of just catching a bathroom graffiti artist or exam cheater. This was much more serious.

To cover his nervousness, Dan adjusted his fine strands of hair, nodded curtly, and crooked his finger for Aaron and Amanda to follow him. Chuck scratched the back of his ear, then sniffed his fingers, with a bewildered expression and watched them venture down the long hallway.

After about ten minutes, Aaron began to regain awareness of his surroundings. He was sitting on the bench outside Principal Parker's office, and the nuances of the hallway hit him with a welcome force of authority. Cool and dark, the hall was usually intimidating, but today it was calming and welcoming. A cocoon to hide and recompose himself, collect his thoughts, assess the damage. He looked down at the torn knee of his jeans. His mud-caked nails slowly felt the edge of the bench beneath him. It was cool as ice, too. His legs had fallen asleep. Then, Steve popped into his head, falling down... Replaying over and over…

"Aaron." Amanda sat down, patting him on the leg, breaking his trance. "He's on the way. It'll just be-"

Aaron pulled away from Amanda and pushed up to his feet. Shaky at first, but now feeling refreshed after the peace and quiet of this chilled sanctuary. He rubbed at a scratch on his hand as he looked anxiously down the hallway. "Why are we waiting?"

"Because we need to wait for Carl to…"

"We need to go find Mikey right now!" Aaron snapped, finding his voice at its normal volume again. He shot a determined glare at Amanda. That could be him out there. Running from a killer's bullets. *Do something.*

"You can't just go, Aaron," she said. But, it was too late. Aaron steamed down the hallway. He didn't run all this way to sit on his behind and waste more time. "Aaron, wait," she called after him, following as he power-walked away. They sped by Chuck as he was hauling a roll of plastic sheeting and dragging it inside the library.

Amanda caught hold of Aaron's forearm, slowing him down. "You don't know who or what's out there, Aaron."

"I don't care. He could be dying!" Aaron wrenched his arm free and kept walking. "I can't believe I just left them out there. Did nothing."

Ahead of them, Dan was pushing open the main doors to greet Carl. "Did you find them?"

With a shake of the head, Carl replied, "Not yet."

Aaron, incensed, sliced between Carl and Dan, shoving the door open to leave.

"Hey, I need to take you down to the station for a full statement…"

The door slammed shut. Aaron was gone.

eleven

Frustration constricting his chest and pulsing at his temples, Aaron was about ready to run again. Where? Who knows. He'd just rather be doing something. Anything. Not sitting around talking about what happened, what he saw.

Carl's hand clamped like a vice onto Aaron's shoulder, turning Aaron around to face him, Amanda, and the school. Aaron cringed to be looking at that stupid building again. This was supposed to be his oasis. But, after chasing it, turned out it was more of a mirage. He needed help, not concerned adults with all their questions.

"Where do you think you're going?" Carl barked. He didn't like to chase kids, and Aaron was no exception.

"The robbers shot Steve and maybe Mike by now, too. If you're not going to do your job then…"

"How do you know it was them?"

"I saw him shoot his partner and then he shot Steve and… and…" Suddenly overcome with emotion, Aaron swallowed hard and looked down at his shuffling feet. Eyes stinging, the heat of tears on his cheek. Amanda quickly moved to Aaron and put a comforting arm around him before he completely lost it.

"It's okay, Aaron. Calm down. Carl's not the enemy here," said Amanda, flashing a meaningful look at Carl, then back to Aaron. "How about we all go out there and have a look around together? Would that be alright?"

"Amanda…" Carl's voice had a chastising tone.

Amanda retaliated in kind with a firm "Carl."

Carl sighed and pointed to his cruiser. He opened the back seat. Aaron and Amanda slid inside.

Principal Parker emerged from the school, looking from the cruiser to Carl. He flapped his arms. "Officer, should I call the parents?"

"That's not necessary, Mister Parker. The station will handle all that. Just go on back inside... We've got it covered. Just stay put in case the missing boy comes over here. Okay?"

Inside the cruiser, Aaron felt like a perp. The seats were worn and a corner was ripped with pieces of foam pecked out. He looked out the window at the tree-laden parking lot, as the radio crackled to life.

Carl opened the driver's door and sidled in. Tremblay's voice blazed over the radio speaker: "Your ears on, Carl?"

"I got you, Sheriff," Carl said, pulling the microphone to his lips. He twisted the key in the ignition and the cruiser roared to life.

"Where you at?"

"Leaving the school now. I'm bringing the kid. And..." Carl glanced over at Amanda, "company." She poked her tongue out and crinkled her nose at his label.

The cruiser rolled out of the high school parking lot. Aaron felt a knot raveling in his stomach as he knew they were heading back to where he had escaped, where Steve was gunned down, and where Mike was probably wounded - or dead.

They sped past the vast football field and bleachers surrounding the school, as Aaron pondered what they would find at their destination. The ride out of town seemed interminably long, in complete silence, and made all the more unbearable by the uncomfortable seating, compared to the cushy limousine that Aaron was accustomed to traveling in. He blinked heavy eyelids and watched as they left behind the last row of porched houses, each candy-colored house a carbon copy of the one before, reaching the end of the paved road.

"Turn here," Aaron said.

Carl looked into the rear-view; Aaron was tense. He steered down the wooded path, and after a few bends; they pulled in just a few strides from the hood of Tremblay's cruiser, which was parked in the opposite direction, facing up the hill. Aaron swallowed as he glanced out the window, thinking of the white van that was once here, starting this whole goddamn mess in the first place.

Suddenly, the door opened and Aaron lost his arm rest, his elbow slipping. He almost fell, exhausted, from the cruiser, but Carl suddenly gripped his upper arm, holding Aaron in place with a rough grip. Aaron looked up at Carl, who was signaling for him to get out while pulling on his arm. Aaron looked at Carl and looked at his arm pointedly. Carl released his tight grip, and Aaron and Amanda stepped out of the cruiser, both showing signs of anticipation.

"Stay here," Carl said to Amanda with a stern glare.

"I'm a big girl, Carl. I can…"

"It might not be safe, babe." Carl tried to turn on the charm, but he didn't have much in him. Instead, he managed a scornful expression and a cutesy whine, "Please? For me?"

Amanda nodded before he could say something stupid like *pretty please with sugar on top*. "And what am I supposed to do?"

"Suck on a lollipop," Carl winked at her. "There's a couple in the glove box."

So, instead of following, Amanda folded her arms in a huff and leaned against Carl's cruiser. Carl walked into the woods with Aaron at his side. Aaron looked around the woods, disoriented. "I'm not exactly sure where it is from here," Aaron murmured, trying to decipher the labyrinth of trees.

"Sheriff? You around?" Carl yelled.

"Over here," Tremblay boomed, not far away.

"Come on," Carl said, taking Aaron's arm and leading him into the bushes in the direction of Tremblay.

Aaron's feet were struggling to keep up with Carl, getting caught on branches and roots. "Yeah, I'm coming, I'm coming." His eyes widened as he recognized the clearing up ahead. He was there. The campsite.

Yet, when Carl and Aaron stepped out of the woods; the scene wasn't how Aaron had left it. He saw the fire pit, and the overturned canoe – but Jake, the bearded man's body had disappeared.

"Did you move him already?" Aaron said, increasingly anxious and confused.

"Who?" Carl said.

"The body. The dead guy." Aaron walked over to the canoe, scanning the ground for any sign of life, or death. There were only a smattering of leaves, sticks and twigs. No body. No blood.

"Where was he?" Carl asked thoughtfully.

Aaron pointed next to the canoe. "Right here."

Carl looked left and right. "Maybe he wasn't dead."

"I saw him die! It was right here!" Aaron exploded excitedly, kicking the canoe with a loud thud.

A twig cracked as Tremblay wandered out of the bushes where Steve and Mike had been hiding. The sheriff slowly ambled toward Carl and Aaron, looking at the ground intently as he approached. He bent down once to inspect a leaf, picking it up and slowly twirling it in front of his face. Tremblay shrugged, dropped the leaf, and looked directly at Aaron through his aviator sunglasses.

Aaron, steadied by the sheriff's presence, stopped overreacting and steadied himself against the side of the canoe.

Tremblay pulled the sunglasses from his face, turned to stare at Carl for a moment, and then redirected his attention to Aaron.

"There's no sign of blood or any sort of foul play that I can see," Tremblay finally said, breaking the silence.

"What do you mean? How can that…" Aaron stammered.

Carl cut Aaron off, saying, "Tell us again exactly what you saw. From the beginning."

Letting out a sigh, Aaron looked down at the ground where Jake's body had bled out. Not a speck of blood. The dirt appeared to be freshly raked under the leaves.

"You were standing in the bushes over there and then you saw…" Carl said, starting Aaron's story for him, while Tremblay stepped closer to the canoe, bending down to examine it.

"No, I was underneath the canoe."

"Underneath it?"

"Yeah. It was flipped over the other way," Aaron explained.

Tremblay straightened, meeting Aaron eye to eye. "What did he look like?"

"He had a beard and I… I… it all went by so fast."

Resting a large hand on Aaron's shoulder, a crooked crevasse formed between Tremblay's nose and chin. After a second, Aaron realized that Tremblay was attempting to smile at him. "It's okay, son, you're not in any trouble here."

"What about the shooter?" Carl spat, impatiently.

Aaron shook his head slowly. "I didn't get a good look at him." Tremblay's eyes shifted to Carl and they momentarily exchanged a suspicious glance, which Aaron caught out of the corner of his field of vision. He looked up abruptly, with a flash of anger. "I'm not lying!"

Carl raised his arms defensively, with a sincere smile that Aaron sensed was merely meant to humor him. Just that crazy

Stevens kid, making up tall tales, is what they must've been thinking. Probably wants to step out of his old man's shadow. Tough on him, too, with all this closing the mill business. Let's nod, make him happy, and go back home for dinner.

Aaron bit his lip, "Maybe Mike and Steve got a better look... Steve!" Suddenly, he charged out of Tremblay and Carl's reach, crossing the campsite at a gallop. The fire pit was on his left, and it was raked as well – empty of any ashes and incriminating evidence. "I'm not lying! Or crazy!" Aaron called over his shoulder as he raced into the woods.

"Hey, kid, come back here!" Carl said, following after Aaron, with Tremblay close behind him.

Aaron found himself running through the very woods he had just fled, only this time in the opposite direction. Potentially towards danger.

twelve

A voice crackled over the radio hanging on Tremblay's belt: "Sheriff Tremblay. Do you read me?"

With a snort, Tremblay stopped in his tracks and removed his radio to answer the call. Ahead of him, Carl and Aaron disappeared on their forage into the forest. "Go ahead."

"I've got Mister Stevens here and he'd like to speak to you about…"

"Tell him I'm busy right now," Tremblay said, putting his sunglasses back on, over his slitted eyes.

"I heard that," Derek Stevens could be heard in the background at the dispatch office.

Tremblay lowered the radio. "Christ."

Tremblay rubbed his temples with one hand and tried to find his Zen, but it was difficult. Given the history between Derek Stevens and himself, Tremblay found it very difficult to talk to the man.

Back when Tremblay was seeking election for the post of Sheriff, Stevens doubted that Tremblay could do the job. And he wasn't quiet about it. Stevens talked to every high-end official in the town about his doubts, making secretive phone calls that cast doubt on Tremblay's drive and abilities. Or so it has been rumored numerous times to Tremblay by many trusty sources.

Even so, the town prevailed against all of Stevens' claims and elected Tremblay ten years ago. Stevens never backed down nor apologized, and Tremblay never confronted the man. Instead, all of their communication has been tense, frosty and overly-formal.

Tremblay finished his brief trek down memory lane. He composed himself, whipped off his sunglasses, and raised the radio again. Tremblay spat into the radio, "Okay, put him on."

On the other side of the clump of trees, Aaron was running, with Carl hot on his heels. For the second time that day, Aaron ducked and weaved between branches, and leapt broken trunks and ditches. He was agile. He knew the woods better than Carl, who was trailing behind him now. But Aaron was also tired and thirsty and about ready to snap in two, mentally and physically. What happened to his friends?

As he reached a small clearing, Aaron started to slow. He wiped away tears streaming along the sides of his face, into his ears. Kicking at the long grass in frustration, Aaron kept hidden while he kept an eye out for Carl.

Then he heard Carl's voice, not far from his position. "Look, Aaron, I'm not saying you didn't see something out here, but put yourself in our shoes and look at it from our side for a minute."

Holding his breath, Carl waited for a response. "I'm not lying!" Aaron shouted, sounded like he was somewhere to the right.

Carl veered in that direction, treading lightly, trying not to make a lot of noise. Crack. Clumsy oaf broke a damn branch. He tried to cover his mistake by talking some more: "Hold on. I didn't say you were. What I am saying though is we can only investigate a crime if there's evidence of one and, well..."

"I know what I saw. Someone must have taken the bodies."

Carl's face appeared strained as he attempted to locate Aaron's voice, which seemed to be bouncing off every tree. "Then there's no sense wasting any more time looking for them out here, right?"

"Hey!" Aaron felt himself being yanked backwards. He let out a surprised yelp and carouselled around to see Carl, who was now resting his arm around Aaron's shoulders.

Carl began to lead Aaron away, keeping his arm firmly closed around him, squeezing a little too tightly. Aaron had no opportunity to escape again, and he slumped against Carl in defeat.

"We need to look somewhere else." Aaron had spent every last ounce of 'fight' on this mad dash, and he was about ready to relinquish the reins of the search to someone else. But, there were so many questions and fears rattling around his head. What about the money?

Walking back to the wooded path, Aaron stepped over a plank that was covered with a layer of dirt; below it was the hole where Jake hid the other backpack.

Amanda straightened from her leaning gait to meet Aaron and Carl as they approached the cruisers. Her face was etched with concern, and she smiled for Aaron's benefit. Aaron was never happier to see a familiar face than now in his exhaustion.

Carl led Aaron to the tail end of the cruiser, and Aaron sat on the bumper. He kneaded the back of his neck and stared off into space, tired and worried.

Carl seemed satisfied that Aaron wouldn't try another cross-country run through the woods again, so he turned to Amanda.

She leaned forward and tried to read Carl's expression. Exasperated to find no clues in his poker face and no forth-coming words, she asked, "So?"

"We didn't find anything," Carl said, looking away.

"Nothing? At all?" Amanda looked over at Aaron, who was still posed in a slightly comatose stare. He looked stricken and shocked. Amanda looked back at Carl and asked again, "Nothing?"

Carl shook his head "no" and glanced over to Tremblay's cruiser. Behind the wheel, the shiny-lensed eyes were watching them as the Sheriff conversed with the radio. Tremblay waved Carl over.

Amanda stared at Carl and Tremblay as Carl walked away. After a moment, she shrugged and turned to Aaron, looking him directly in the eyes. She placed a hand on his shoulder. Startled, Aaron's unfocused stare began to focus on his teacher. With concern lacing her voice, Amanda asked, "What's going on, Aaron?"

Aaron wiped at his dirty face in frustration and answered, "I don't know."

"Did you even see something out here or is this just another of your…"

"You don't believe me either? Thanks a lot, Miss Becker." Aaron looked away from Amanda and scuffed his toe against the dirt.

Carl was back. "The Sheriff wants to talk to you," he said, with a serious tone. "He just wants to ask you some more questions about what happened."

Sucking in his courage, Aaron knew that he would need to dig into his reserves; Tremblay wasn't done with him yet. Without another word, he headed for Tremblay's cruiser. Amanda and Carl watched him walk away like a man on death row, on his way to the chair.

Aaron stopped at Tremblay's window. He looked down at the Sheriff, who stared straight ahead, stone-faced.

"Get in," Tremblay said, through the open window. He pointed to the back seat.

Aaron slid into the back, closing the door just as Tremblay started the engine. "I thought you were just going to ask me some questions," Aaron remarked, trying – and failing – to appear unconcerned.

"At the station, not here."

Aaron's stomach sank, along with his courage. They were going downtown.

The cruiser pulled away, leaving Carl and Amanda arguing at the edge of the woods.

thirteen

The red glowing tinge of a setting sun bounced off the roof of Tremblay's cruiser as it sharked through the streets of Pineville, with sirens in the place of a predatory fin. The cruiser chased the smaller fish, the civilian cars, to their hiding places on the side of the road. As the cruiser swam past, the drivers breathed sighs of relief that the sirens were not meant to capture them. At least not for today.

Aaron watched this game of justice and civility, cat and mouse, shark and fish. He found it unfair. "The Law" could force people to obey traffic symbols but could do nothing for his two friends.

About to burst with frustration and concern for his friends, Aaron tapped on the wire cage between Tremblay and himself. Tremblay turned almost imperceptibly. Without saying a word or looking at Aaron, Aaron knew he had the Sheriff's full attention.

Aaron considered what he was about to say. Did he really want to tell the Sheriff about the money? That he knew about the bank robbery? Would that make him a suspect? He opened his mouth to talk, just as the cruiser prowled into the parking area and stopped at the groaning mouth of the station's main doors. Tremblay flicked off the engine and adjusted the rear-view mirror to stare at Aaron, sizing him up.

"You do realize making a false report is a serious crime," Tremblay's words shot with intent to wound.

"But I didn't! I can prove it all happened just like I said," Aaron pleaded, still clinging to any remnants of fight left in the depths of his body and soul.

Suddenly, Tremblay was the one who appeared to be cautious. "Prove it? How?"

Aaron drew in a sharp intake of breath. "I found the bank money."

Tremblay immediately stiffened and turned to lasso Aaron with a steely glare. "The bank money?" His voice was different, strange, urgent, concerned, excited. Not the cardboard cutout Sheriff who talked about drugs in class. This was a motivated individual, with goals, dreams, aspirations, fears. Tremblay was human after all.

"Yeah," Aaron said, feeling like he was finally getting someone on his side. Maybe Tremblay, of all people, believed him.

"If this is some sort of..."

"I'm telling the truth. It was in a backpack under the canoe."

"Then why the hell didn't you say something back there?" Tremblay cursed, about to start the engine again.

"Because it's not back there anymore."

Tremblay froze. "Where is it, Aaron?"

"I brought it to the school with me."

Tremblay cranked the key in the ignition so fast that Aaron thought the entire car might flip over with the sheer breakneck momentum of the hand's turn. Then Tremblay slammed the cruiser into gear, pulled away from the station and zipped out on to Main Street.

The cruiser sped down Main Street at breakneck speed, with the sirens blaring and Tremblay cursing the entire way back to the school. Arriving, the Sheriff screeched to a halt in front of the school.

Back at the entrance to the high school, Amanda and Carl were hugging, making up, not expecting to see Tremblay's cruiser lining up beside Carl's. Their night wasn't over yet.

Aaron flew forward in response to the sheriff's abrupt halt. Carl tucked his hands into his pockets and stepped away from Amanda, as he watched the cruiser grind to a halt.

Dispatch crackled on the radio: "Sheriff, you still on?"

Tremblay put the cruiser in park, cursed and grabbed the radio. "Go ahead."

"Mister Stevens is back."

"My dad?" Aaron balked, as Tremblay brought the mic up to his mouth to speak.

Aaron leaned forward to the mesh-wall separating him from Tremblay. He clasped the tips of his fingers around the mesh and plastered his face to the metal. With desperation, he pleaded, "Please don't tell him I took his money. He'll kill me if he knew I had something to do with this."

"Where the hell are you?" Derek's furious tones were unmistakable, masked unsuccessfully in a cold, steely and distant business voice; Aaron knew them too well. "You said ten minutes, Tremblay. I have other things to do besides sit around waiting for you! I want to know what…"

With a light clink, Carl tapped on Tremblay's window with the end of a lollipop as Aaron listened to his Dad drone on; hot air, as usual. "Everything all right, Sheriff?" Carl said, peering inside.

fourteen

Amanda walked into the school with Aaron, leaving Carl and Tremblay to their discussions in the parking lot. The door clicked shut behind them and a flustered-looking Principal Parker jangled his keys as he approached the pair. "Miss Becker, I was just about to lock up. Any luck?"

The door clicked again behind Carl as he slipped into the school, causing all three to turn in his direction. "Okay, Aaron, the Sheriff just told me. Can you show me?"

Aaron nodded and set off down the hall with Carl beside him, Amanda behind and Principal Parker trailing at the back of the pack, still appearing puzzled and out of the loop. "What happened out there, Carl? What did you find out?"

"It's under control, Mister Parker," Carl said with a flippant tone, a purposeful glare in his eyes.

"What's under control? You're not telling me anything," Principal Parker barked, getting his back up.

"Yeah, Carl," Amanda chimed in, causing Carl to flick his eyes at her, hoping to silence her sharp tongue.

The fiery embers in Amanda's eyes told Carl that this wasn't over. "Look, Amanda, you really need to leave this to us and not get any more involved," he snapped, a final shot.

"They're my students. Of course I'm going to get in-volved," Amanda hissed at him, with no plans of letting Carl get in the last word. She'd put up with his attitude for too long. He was always dismissing her out of hand, especially in front of other people, including her students, and now her boss, Principal Parker. *How dare he treat me like a second-class citizen.* Not today, not again.

Carl didn't have time to put Amanda in her place, though. He kept moving, focused on Aaron, as they arrived outside the library. Could this kid really have the evidence, sitting neatly tucked beneath a few rolls of plastic? Apparently not, if Aaron's sickly gasp was anything to go by. His face was pale as a sheet when he turned to his followers. "It's gone!"

"What?" Carl rasped.

Aaron pointed to the empty spot, where just a box of rags and some assorted tools remained strewn haphazardly on the ground.

"I stashed it right here."

Carl frowned and pursed his lips, before curling them into a displeased grimace. "Now I suppose you're going to tell me it just vanished into thin air - like the bodies did?"

Aaron felt the bottom fall out of his stomach, like a weight crashing at his feet.

Principal Parker gruffly pushed past Amanda. "Bodies? What the devil is-"

Glancing at the 'Danger' sign beside the doors, Aaron's heart skipped a beat. "Maybe... maybe someone moved it?"

Aaron's suggestions fell on deaf ears, as Carl grabbed the boy by the arm and yanked him away from the library. "If your nose was Pinocchio's it would be as long as my…"

"Carl!" Amanda cried, cutting Carl's remark short.

"I'm done listening to his stories," Carl spluttered, the indignation getting caught in his throat.

"But, I really found…"

"Shut up! You've wasted enough of our time." Carl's 'good cop' veneer had slipped, revealing a hot-headed and frustrated man who's had enough crap for one day. Amanda shot him a warning glance, but Carl didn't care. He knew a wild goose chase when he saw one. Missing money, missing bodies. There was a real search to do but this kid was just wasting time.

Principal Parker slowly coughed and interjected in the silent aftermath of Carl's outburst. "What's going on? Aaron?"

Aaron swallowed and began to answer: "I found the…"

"I said shut up!" Carl's voice was sharp and fired at Aaron with a violent velocity.

"But…" Aaron's face was strained and weary. Why wouldn't anybody believe him?

Carl pulled a cell phone from his pocket and flipped it open. Yet, Principal Parker raised an index finger in polite protest. "That won't work in here."

"Why not?"

"We installed a 'no cell phone' system this year. Too many students were spending all their time texting and so forth..."

Carl didn't wait for Parker to finish his rambling thought and instead walked away, down the hallway. "Wait here. I'll be right back," he said, directed at Amanda. "I have to call the Sheriff."

Principal Parker shook his head, clearly feeling vexed by his sudden lack of authority in his own school. Watching Carl leave, Parker touched Amanda on the arm, snapping her out of a glazed expression. "Look, I have to finish locking up, and then I'm heading home for a bit," he told her. "Call me with an update, if *they* tell you anything." He rolled his eyes, as she nodded back at him.

As Parker ambled down the corridor, out of view and ear-shot, Amanda leaned towards Aaron, in a friendly, collegial way. "What did you find, Aaron?"

Aaron studied her face. "What?"

"Carl said to show him something."

"The money," he said, clearly and loudly. Triumphantly the words came out of his mouth. Finally somebody wanted to hear what he had to say. Somebody was actually listening. "I found the money the robbers took from the bank."

fifteen

Amanda was quiet for a moment or two. "Oh my God," she muttered absent-mindedly. "Aaron, this is important - where's the money now?"

"It was right there…" Aaron pointed to the empty space of floor, just as the library doors burst open with a loud slam – a monstrous hulk clambering toward them, part Darth Vader, part Sponge Bob Squarepants. Amanda screamed, before realizing that what first appeared to be a Space Monster was in fact Chuck in a large bright-yellow biohazard suit, with an air-filtered helmet.

"Jesus, Chuck!" Amanda exclaimed, holding her heart as if it might explode.

"Sorry, guys," Chuck said in a muffled hiss as he pulled the helmet off, in a fine cloud of dust, unmasking a bemused grin.

Amanda stepped back, covering her mouth with her hand. She sure as hell wasn't paid enough to inhale any toxins. Yet, Aaron leaned forward, peering into the library to see a bunch of Chuck's tools and materials scattered around.

"Did you find a green bag out here?" Aaron asked, impatiently.

"A green bag?" Chuck vacantly repeated Aaron's words.

"A backpack," Aaron clarified.

Chuck shook his head slowly. "No, I don't think so..." He turned back to the doors and walked into the library. "Come on in - it's still okay to breathe in here... for now."

Amanda looked uncertain, but followed Aaron inside regardless.

Outside the school, Carl was leaning against the door to his cruiser, with his cell phone pressed to his ear. "I think we should just take him back to the..."

Suddenly, the voice on the other end of the phone cut Carl off. Carl cleared his throat and frowned. "But, what for? It's obviously not here... Okay, okay, I'll look around a bit more and then head over."

Carl hit the red 'end call' button and slipped the phone back into his pocket. There was a cloud over his head. It seemed like the goose-chase wasn't over yet. And now he had to look for a bag that a kid – a born-liar, just like his old man – says is hidden in the school all the while facing Amanda's scornful, needy glances.

Kicking the ground, Carl took a deep breath and went to re-enter the school building. Gripping the handle, he pulled, but the door wouldn't budge. "What the...?"

Carl slammed his fist on the glass. Locked out. He turned around just in time to see a car turning out of the parking lot. "Mister Parker?! Amanda! Where are you going?" Carl screamed in vain. The car was already speeding away.

Back in the library, Amanda walked cautiously amongst the disarray. She craned her neck upwards. Every third or so ceiling tile was missing - black holes staring down on her - with long sheets of thin plastic cascading down from each square. In the middle of the room, a ladder ascended into a larger ceiling opening. Amanda glanced around at the plastic film, covering the book shelves. All the spines and titles were blurry and obscured.

On the ground, Aaron noticed the plastic rolls that Chuck had moved. A green blur was amongst the plastic film. Aaron immediately recognized the backpack's shape and size. "Found it."

Rushing over, Amanda hovered behind Aaron as he lifted the backpack out of the plastic rolls. Ceremoniously, he unzipped the bag and, right on schedule, he revealed its contents - stuffed to the brim with bundles of cash.

"Holy shit," Amanda gasped.

"Told ya."

"Is that it?" Chuck asked, angling to see past Amanda.

Aaron zipped the backpack closed. The show was over. "Yeah. Thanks for your, uh, help."

Chuck nodded. "Then you two need to get along. It's going to get too dangerous in here. Unless you're a pro, like me." Putting on his helmet with a quirky grin, Chuck climbed back up the ladder into the ceiling cavity.

Aaron and Amanda exchanged glances, almost reading each other's minds, and headed for the doors - the backpack tightly grasped in Aaron's hand. Feeling vindicated, his cargo suddenly felt lighter.

Once outside in the corridor, Amanda whispered sharply, "I can't believe you took it."

"It's my dad's."

"What do you mean?" she asked, puzzled.

"He just deposited it for some deal about the mill."

"Really? Wow! So the rumors are true?" Amanda said, with a sideways look.

They stopped by Amanda's classroom and she picked up her purse, slinging it over her shoulder as Aaron waited in the corridor. He was shuffling his feet when she returned. "Speaking of rumors - can I ask you something, Miss Becker?"

"Sure," she replied, suddenly looking at Aaron closely for the first time in hours. The scratches on his face. A small scab of caked blood around a knick on his chin. He looked literally beaten up by the day's events. Yet his eyes were gleaming with triumph. He found the backpack. He proved the adults wrong. And now here he was, standing in front of her, with a question to ask. "What do you want to know?"

"Are you dating Carl?"

Amanda nodded. "For almost a year now, why?"

"It's just that I heard Steve mention it; that's all."

Amanda smiled. "Well, you need to tell Steve to mind his own..." Her voice trailed off. She put her hand on Aaron's arm, squeezing it. "Oh, I'm sorry, Aaron."

The light was disappearing, as the sun dipped below the horizon. It was time for the stars and moon to own the sky. A faint twinkling began to sprinkle the murky navy-blue canvas above Carl and his cruiser. He was about ready to throw his cell phone as he reached Amanda's voicemail for the tenth time.

"I told you to wait for me, Amanda. What the hell are you guys doing?"

Suddenly, the cruiser's radio crackled to life, bristling with the familiar voice of Tremblay. "Carl. You there?"

"Call me back," Carl barked, ending his call abruptly. Reaching into the cruiser, Carl found the radio's mic. "Go ahead, Sheriff."

"Those kids' parents called in. I need you to head over and take their statements."

"I thought you wanted me to..."

"Listen, Carl. When I tell you to do something, you do it." Tremblay's words were sharp, and stuck in the air like darts in a dartboard.

"Yes, sir... I'm on the way." Carl slid into his cruiser, muttering under his breath. "Asshole."

Only seconds later, Amanda pushed open the main doors, with Aaron a few steps behind her dragging the backpack. She was just in time to see the receding taillights of Carl's cruiser.

"That's weird. Where's he going?" she said, distantly.

The glowing red streaks disappeared into the night. "He must have got word about Steve and Mike," Aaron said looking up.

"Yeah, maybe," Amanda murmured, catching the door before it locked shut behind them. "Come on." They headed back inside, Aaron lugging the heavy bag through the doors.

A new light suddenly illuminated the parking lot. The interior light of a vehicle parked in the shadows, as the driver opened his door, stepping out; the gravel crunching ominously under his boot.

Aaron and Amanda were half way up the corridor, when the sound of the main door rattling, locked, caused them to spin around. "He came back," Amanda said, nodding to Aaron.

Aaron sighed, turning on his heels. "Here we go again." Pulling the backpack around to face the opposite direction, he started back towards the main doors, where the rattling had increased in volume and force.

In the pale light of the moon, Tremblay was waiting for them. The glint on his Sheriff's badge was luminescent compared to his dark silhouette, as were the whites of his eyes, looking up from beneath the brim of his hat.

Without verifying who was at the door, Amanda pushed her hip into the door, as she flipped and broke the lock's seal with her hands, before shouldering the rest of the door to push it wide open for Tremblay. Tremblay stepped through the doorway and Amanda gasped, slightly taken aback to see the craggy-faced old man, instead of Carl's rugged but considerably smoother features. "Oh, Sheriff, I thought you were..."

Tremblay pushed past Amanda without a word and set his sights on Aaron, who stood a few steps beyond Amanda, the backpack lying at his side.

"Is that the money?" Tremblay croaked.

"What?" Amanda asked, a crease forming between her eyes.

"Yeah," Aaron snipped back with a sarcastic tone.

Tremblay's eyes slitted, and the iridescent whites thinned around his pupils, as the lids held the two pinholes implausibly steady on Aaron's face, like chopsticks grasping a pair of jet-black olives.

Aaron perceived something dangerous in the embrace of Tremblay's glare. Then he noticed that Tremblay's hand was moving as he stared at him; it wandered along his belt, feeling its path, until reaching a set of handcuffs.

Clink. The cuffs were unclipped and fell at Tremblay's feet. The same sound clinked inside Aaron's head – the penny had dropped, too. As he looked down, he saw the sheriff's pant cuffs were resting on top of fancy alligator skin boots still caked with mud from the woods – whether it was from returning with Aaron or earlier in the day when he killed Jake, Aaron wasn't sure. However, he was sure that this man, Tremblay, was a killer and a thief, and he planned to do both again – right now.

sixteen

Tremblay bent down and retrieved the cuffs that slipped from his grasp, finally taking his eyes off Aaron.

Aaron's mouth opened into a small 'o'. "What's the matter, Aaron?" Amanda asked, noticing a transformation in his previous demeanor.

His eyes flashing from the alligator boots, to Tremblay, and back to Amanda; Aaron couldn't find the words quick enough.

Suddenly, Tremblay stood, turned, and snapped the cuffs around the door posts. Locking them all inside the school.

"Run, Miss Becker!" Aaron cried. With a hefty swing, he tossed the backpack's strap over his shoulder and hightailed it down the hallway.

Amanda appeared puzzled and dazed. "Aaron?" She watched Aaron run, and then turned to reconsider the cuffed door. "What are you doing, Sheriff?"

Tremblay was cool… cold. "I want my money."

Backing away, she too realized what was happening. "Oh my God..."

Taking one large step forward, Tremblay grabbed the collar of Amanda's dress, brusquely pulling her close to him. He held her for a moment and looked deep into her eyes before coldly stating, "Get that kid back here or I'll…"

Before Tremblay could finish his thought, Amanda delivered a devastating kick between his legs, silencing his threat and allowing her to break free from his grasp. Letting out a groaning wheeze, Tremblay crumpled to his knees.

Amanda ran like she hadn't run in a long time. She had trained in track and field when she was a young girl, but she didn't even like the running machine at the gym anymore. Yet, today, she was making an exception. Running for her life.

She felt the chilling rush of air, as the walls of the corridor turned into a gray tunnel, all the framed pictures of tree-planting ceremonies and school teams with their awards, blurring into a single color.

Then she heard it. The gunshot, echoing along the corridor behind her. She reached the end of the hallway and a chunk of concrete exploded from the wall in front of her, narrowly missing her head.

Next, she heard her own scream, as she whipped around the corner, out of reach from Tremblay and his bullets.

Bumping into Aaron, Amanda involuntarily screamed again. Her adrenaline was through the roof, like her heart would never stop beating this hard. Aaron grabbed her arm, and she felt the walls slowing down again and the colors and details returned. "We can hide in here," Aaron said to her, pointing to the doors to the library.

"We need to call Carl," Amanda responded, out of breath.

Both Aaron and Amanda suddenly turned toward the sound of Tremblay's boots, pounding up the corridor at a good clip.

Aaron pulled open the door to the library and shoved Amanda inside. "I'll call."

Before she could argue with him, Aaron was moving. With the backpack on his shoulder, he set off towards Principal Parker's office. Not far away, Aaron could still hear the metronome-like tick-tock of Tremblay's footsteps, getting louder and firmer with every tick and every tock.

Throwing down the backpack, Aaron reached the outer office, the switchboard. Aaron quickly pulled the chair out of his way and scooped up the telephone receiver. Tapped 9-1-1. He listened intently. Nothing. He tapped 9-1-1 again. "Come on, come on..." he yelped impatiently.

Aaron started pushing random buttons, flipping a couple of switches. A light illuminated.

"Please, please..." Aaron chanted in prayer.

He punched a number into the keypad. Waiting. Listening. Finally, Aaron smacked the receiver down onto the switchboard, and then put it back to his ear.

"Somebody answer!" he cursed.

Aaron gave up, dropped the receiver and ran for the door, with the first fresh beads of perspiration appearing on his forehead.

Inside the library, now the sun had set and made the space a shadowy cavern. The reflection of moon beams from the corner skylight on the plastic-covered book shelves offered the only semblance of light to navigate the room. Amanda shuffled in, partially scared of her own shadow, and with her trust in tatters. She passed a water tank, almost knocking it over, and ducked around a sheet of hanging plastic. Arriving at the circulation desk, she stumbled over Chuck's tools making a racket as they clattered together. *Shhhh*. She pleaded with the tools, but they weren't cooperating with her.

Noticing a crowbar in the pile, Amanda bent over to pick it up – completely oblivious to Chuck, who poked his helmeted-head from the gap in the ceiling beside the ladder, to see what made all the noise. Not noticing any movement, he retreated back into the hole, like a whack-a-mole.

Amanda, entrenched into her position behind the circulation desk, clutched the crowbar tightly, her knuckles turning white.

Then a soft rustle came from somewhere in the library. Amanda's neck snapped straight, her eyebrows rose, and her muscles tensed. *What the hell was that?* She raised her head slowly to look above the desk. A hanging sheet of plastic was swaying from a light breeze.

She sniffed at her tension, and opened her purse, rummaging through it for another weapon. The only thing she found was a pack of cigarettes. Might calm the nerves. Amanda shook the pack, and the silence of the empty pack rattled her nerves even more. "Damnit," she whispered to herself. Then she noticed it – a shape, tall and dark, behind a sheet of plastic. Her hand clapped over her mouth, stifling a gasp.

On the other side of the sheet, Tremblay was equipped with his Colt raised, and his ears pricked up at her gasp. Found her.

Tremblay cocked the gun's hammer with his thumb and the loud click sent Amanda into a wave of panic. She held her breath, turning toward the shape with the crowbar in her hand. Do or die. Then it happened - Chuck dropped a tool in the ceiling cavity.

Tremblay sprung like a viper, whirling around and fanning the trigger as he fired into the ceiling tiles at three different spots. The bullets ventilated the roof above them, in a flurry of dust and crumbs.

Aaron arrived at the library doors just in time to hear the shooting. He threw his arms over his head, ducking for cover. The shots were so piercing and deafening, sending a shockwave through Aaron's body – and his mind. Bringing him back to the woods... Steve... Mike... And now Miss Becker.

Two more shots rang out. Aaron crinkled his eyes. "Oh, God, no..."

Tremblay looked up into the smoking holes he'd made in the ceiling and he waited for another noise. The silence seemed to confirm his kill. That little punk Aaron was a goner. And now he'd take care of Amanda. Leaning towards the circulation desk, Tremblay angled his gun. But Amanda had other plans for Tremblay. *Thwack!*

His nose took the brunt of the impact from the crowbar. Dropping the Colt, it bounced under some of Chuck's materials, falling over a roll of plastic sheeting. Stumbling backwards, blood spurting down his face, Tremblay was reeling from this surprise-attack.

Amanda hit him again and again, until he went down for good. She snatched up her purse, in exchange for the crowbar, and ran out of the library. Leaving Tremblay spread-eagled on the floor, unconscious.

The doors burst open as Aaron started to run again. "Aaron, wait!"

He slammed on the brakes and turned with a smile, relieved to see Amanda rushing toward him, and not Tremblay's imposing frame.

"Holy shit, I thought you were him… I thought he killed you, too."

Amanda hugged Aaron, just as happy to find him in one piece. "I knocked him out."

"You did?" Aaron said, shaking his head, astonished.

Amanda quickly grabbed Aaron's hand and tugged him along with her. "Hurry. Before he wakes up."

Seventeen

Tremblay's eyelids flickered -- then unzipped. Damage report. Blood staining his lip and chin. Pounding headache. Nothing broken, except maybe the nose. Wouldn't be the first time though.

Finding the crowbar at his fingertips, Tremblay used it as a crutch to push himself to his feet. He staggered off balance until he gained his bearings again. Wiped his sore, bloody nose on the back of his sleeve. Then he smashed the crowbar against the desk, in one furious sweep of the arm, letting out an almighty roar. He was pissed as hell. Now they were gonna suffer.

Aaron and Amanda had arrived at the backpack, left outside of Principal Parker's office. "We should give him the money," Aaron said, finally considering surrender.

"What the hell for?" Amanda snipped.

"So he won't slaughter us - what do you think?"

Amanda tapped the weighty backpack with her shoe. "Until Carl gets here, this is the only thing keeping us alive."

With a big swallow, Aaron looked hard at Amanda. "I didn't call him."

"What?" she screeched at a higher pitch than originally intended.

"The phone didn't work."

Amanda couldn't hide the swirling whirlpool of panic in her eyes. She rushed to the switchboard, flipped a switch, picked up the receiver and listened. She then dialed a number, throwing Aaron a look of "what the hell?" It was working. Aaron shrugged. Stupid switchboard. Old quirky technology.

A hobbling Tremblay composed himself, dusted off his clothes, and straightened to his usual gait. Walking tall, he made his way along the corridor. He passed a maintenance room on his left and pushed open the door: empty. He kept walking and then stopped in his tracks. He doubled back.

His eyes scanned the interior of the maintenance room. Some cobwebs in the corner. A mop and bucket. Three electrical junction boxes on the wall. Above the boxes hung a huge map of the school's layout, showing its hallways, two main floors, basement and the two main entrance/exits.

Meanwhile, Amanda anxiously bounced her leg as she sat, talking on the phone. "Please hurry, Carl. We're locked inside the school and Tremblay is after us..."

But her call was being routed from the school to Carl's cell phone voicemail. On the passenger seat of his cruiser, the LCD display of the cell phone was brightly lit, with Amanda's missed call. Just feet away, Carl was interviewing a kid, one of Steve's younger brothers – another wild goose chase.

Amanda sighed as she recorded the last of the most hopeless message she'd ever left in her life. "He wants the money and…"

The lights went out across the whole school building. Pitch black.

The phone was dead, too. Amanda shrieked.

Aaron knew it would only get darker.

eighteen

In a crackle and flash of sparks, Tremblay bashed at the last of the three electrical junction boxes on the wall, snuffing out every light bulb in the building, including the one above his head.

Enveloped in shadows, apart from the last spark's glimmer on his large mouthful of teeth, a slowly widening grin of victory covered his face as Tremblay turned about-face on his cowboy-booted heels and left the room. Hunting for his prey. Hiding somewhere in the inky corridors of the school.

Tremblay's smile was short-lived, however; he accidentally bumped into a large garbage pail of old broken bats and deflated basketballs. With a loud clatter, he toppled over onto all fours before wheezing back onto his feet. A dim emergency light flickered on above him. Just enough of a glow to see the dust on his knees, brush it off, and then keep moving up the hallway, kicking a shriveled basketball out of his path. He passed a door marked 'ROOF' with a sign below it: "WARNING: Door locks from outside."

In the darkness, hands suddenly become lifelines, guiding, feeling every edge and wall. Reaching for the corner of the desk, Amanda's fingers found it and she followed the trail of the desk's ledge, until she saw ahead of her the stuttering glare of emergency lights outside Principal Parker's Office. She moved towards the hazy glow and blinked with relief – until she realized that Aaron was gone, along with the backpack.

"Shit," she cursed, looking up the hallway just as Aaron was about to round the corner into the next hallway. "Aaron? Where are you going?" she hissed, quietly but firmly.

"I have to stash it," he replied, without turning back.

Aaron's eyes darted back and forth, looking high and low for any nooks and crannies that could conceal the backpack. Never before had he noticed how streamlined the old corridors were. No out-of-reach shadows, at a time when darkness could be his only friend.

Suddenly, a shrieking metallic crash came from somewhere in the school. Aaron spun around, still walking, to see Amanda lurching back inside the office. He then looked forward just in time to see the row of lockers - within inches of his eyes. Unable to stop in time, he body-checked the locker door, denting more than his pride, and simultaneously splitting the seam of the backpack in his hands.

Several bundles of cold, hard cash spilled out onto the floor. They seemed to thud loudly as the heavy wads somersaulted to a halt, or at least in Aaron's mind they were as loud as the crash which distracted him in the first place.

Aaron quickly squatted to grab some of the bundles, silencing them with his hands, before shoving them into the torn backpack. One of the paper bands ripped in his haste. A flurry of $100 bills fluttered around him seemingly in slow motion. *Shit.*

Floating down like a feather, a single bill's impact was weirdly explosive, echoing down the corridor. Then the next bill struck the ground with the boom of a thunderclap. Aaron frowned, before realizing that it wasn't the dollars making all the racket. He looked apprehensively back towards the office, where Amanda was hiding.

Tremblay raised the crowbar again, and slammed it down onto the already crippled and steaming switchboard. The phone receiver flipped off the hook, broken in half by the jagged end of the metal bar.

Catching his breath, Tremblay appeared satisfied by his handiwork. He had worked up quite a sweat. Dripping down his nose. A bead suddenly rolled along the bridge and then off to the side, absorbed into his right tear duct. He winced; his eye was stinging. Then, it swiveled around, the other eye followed in synchronicity, scanning the dark room for movement.

Amanda's heart was pounding out of her chest. Behind a partially closed door, she was cramped in close quarters, waiting and listening. It was worse now the noise had stopped. So loud that the silence seemed like an abyss. She wondered if she'd fall into it, and never get out again.

The horrid thud of Tremblay's boot interrupted the peace, kicking the door wide open – stopping just an inch away from Amanda's cheek. There was an almighty crack and crunch of wood on wood - her face rescued by the edge of a coat rack, blocking the door's trajectory.

Amanda bit down hard on her finger, just to stop from screaming. On the other side of the door, Tremblay's silhouette was standing fearsomely wielding the crowbar. He paused, white eyes flickering over the shadows in the office, then he turned abruptly. Gone.

nineteen

Aaron clambered around, scooping up the last of the loose bills. He stuffed them haphazardly into the backpack, but something was tucked down near the bottom, wedged in tight. Aaron wiggled his hand in deep, trying to move the obstruction. Suddenly, his eyes illuminated like a light bulb in that dull corridor.

Pulling out his arm, Aaron looked down at what he was holding - the steely grip on a Colt 45 pistol. "Whoa!" It looked exactly like the one in Tremblay's holster, Aaron thought as he lifted it into the air. Heavier than he imagined. And stinky. Like oil, dirt and smoke.

Aaron took a deep breath, glancing up and down the corridor. Time to make his next move. But what would that be?

With a tiny creak, Amanda pushed the door ajar and slipped around it. Treading carefully, she tiptoed through the office, stepping over the destruction of the switchboard. Then, reaching the doorway to the corridor, Amanda leaned over, slowly, holding her breath, scared to keep her eyes open. Nothing.

Then a sharp pull from behind caused Amanda to let out a wail. Tremblay had grabbed her hair and was yanking her out into the hallway. He pulled her up to his eyeballs, as she scratched and swung at him.

"I've had enough of your shit!" Tremblay barked.

Amanda twisted and cried, as her hair slipped from his grasp, and she dropped to the floor. A marionette after the puppet-master had released the strings. Skittering away from Tremblay on her hands and feet, Amanda was wide-eyed, terrified, and unaware that Tremblay was raising the crowbar to strike again.

He slammed the bar down, narrowly missing her ribs as Amanda rolled out of the way. "Where is he?" Tremblay screamed, interrogating her. He swung again, whacking Amanda's right thigh with the crowbar. The searing pain. She howled.

"I can do this all night, bitch, so you better tell me..."

She whimpered. Tremblay reared back to strike Amanda again when he heard the dangerous 'click' of a cocked gun.

"Drop it, asshole!" The familiar voice of Aaron echoed as he aimed the Colt at the back of Tremblay's head.

Tremblay froze, Amanda looked up. Nobody moved.

"Are you deaf?" Aaron's voice echoed down the corridors. He stepped closer, just a few feet from Tremblay and Amanda, still sprawled on the floor.

Tremblay grimaced and dropped the crowbar. It rattled with a clang.

"Are you alright, Miss Becker?" Aaron said, moving around to be by her side, to face Tremblay's mean gaze. Amanda nodded, easing herself to her feet, rubbing her sore thigh. Her nails were chipped from the fall and clawing; her eyes bled mascara. She found the crowbar with her other hand and lifted it up with her as she stood.

Aaron didn't take his eyes off Tremblay. He kept the Colt trained on him, with a quivering hand; as he took another sidestep over to stand right next to Amanda. Then he steadied the Colt with both hands.

"You do know Daddy's not coming for you, right?" Tremblay finally said.

"Shut up!"

"He's too busy worrying about how he's going to get his 'screw you' to Pineville money back so he can--"

"What are you talking about?" Aaron interjected, his face flushed red.

"Oh, come on, don't play dumb. You know damn well he's going to shut down the mill after he sells it."

"You're wrong. He wouldn't do that."

Tremblay shot Aaron with an accusatory glare. "Wouldn't he?"

Meanwhile, miles away, Carl was leaning against the rear door of his cruiser, looking out across the dark fields, talking on his cell phone. "You're not answering the radio or your cell. Where are you, Jay?" his voice quivered. "Call me back. I have news."

Carl glanced down at the cruiser window behind him, where there was Mike's scared, dirty face pressed against the glass. Scared, dirty, but alive.

Suddenly, Carl noticed the flashing icon on his phone. A little envelope. A voice message. He pressed the button and retrieved it... Not Jay; it was Amanda. *"Please hurry, Carl. We're locked inside the school and Tremblay..."*

"Jesus Christ!" Carl jolted into action, as if an electric shock had injected his heart. Not wasting a second, he whipped around the cruiser to the driver's side.

The engine started. Exhaust blew smoke. Dirt sprayed from the rear tires into the air.

On a mission, the cruiser sped off into the black night.

twenty

Amanda squeezed the crowbar tight in her hand. Aaron tried to look tough with the Colt. In reality, he wasn't the man he wanted to portray. He was a boy mixed up in some serious shit. Could he even handle the recoil on this gun? Would he have to? He'd only pulled a trigger once before.

His Dad's idea of a bonding exercise: hunting for a week at a lonely cabin in the woods. It smelt musty and of dead things. But one of the guys at the mill gave Derek the keys and he dragged Aaron along for some 'quality time.' Time for the boys to talk and forget about work and school. Just be a couple of guys.

It was a disaster as usual. Hardly any talk, except Derek cursing his cellphone reception, and Aaron cursing under his breath at being stuck in the middle of nowhere. Then came the day they shot the deer. Derek bossed Aaron around, telling him how to point a gun, like he's some kind of Desert Storm sniper.

Derek took the first shot and the doe went down. But she was still alive. Needed that kill shot. "Go on, Aaron. Do it. Do it!" Aaron heard his father's words, yet saw the tears in the doe's eyes. He aimed the rifle and looked away. One second, she was alive. Then – BANG! – the doe was dead.

It was very quiet for the rest of that trip. Not a word was spoken. The deer's silence spoke for the both of them.

"Why do you think I put in for a transfer?" Tremblay said, breaking Aaron's train of thought. His beady eyes turned to Amanda. "Surely, Carl must have-"

Amanda suddenly whacked Tremblay in the kneecap with the crowbar. A vicious outburst from a woman who'd had enough.

Tremblay yelped in agony and dropped to the floor, clutching his knee. He looked up, tears in his eyes, like that damn deer – *Why'd she have to be walking through their neck of the woods that day?*

Amanda smashed Tremblay in the temple, a brutal swing, knocking one out of the park. His head crumpled to the floor. Out like a light.

"Come on..." she shouted, grabbing Aaron by the hand.

"But what about...?"

"He's probably dead," she said, pulling Aaron in one hand and carrying the crowbar in the other, droplets of blood on its clawed edge.

Aaron tucked the Colt into his waistband as they hustled down the corridor.

Tremblay moaned heavily as he rolled over. Not dead. Not alive. Somewhere in between. Waiting for a kill shot. Or a resurrection.

twenty one

Amanda led Aaron to the doors of the library. "Why are we coming back here?" he asked, out of breath and perturbed.

She didn't answer him but pulled him through the doors and across the dusty room to the circulation desk. Aaron looked up at the ceiling, riddled with holes, and down at the floor, covered in a fine powder.

Craning her neck, Amanda found what she was searching for. She reached down for her purse, opened it and took out her cell phone.

"I thought they don't work in here."

"They do outside. I'm going to..."

She stopped mid-thought as something dripped onto her nose. She wiped it off quickly with the back of her hand. Red smear on her knuckle. Another droplet landed on her wrist. "What the...?"

Amanda looked up at one of Tremblay's bullet holes. It was bleeding. The pool of red was spreading across the ceiling tile.

Then the god-awful creak of the weight of something signaled it was time to jump out of the way. But it was too late. Chuck's hulking body came crashing through the ceiling, careening down on top of Amanda, creating a heap on the ground.

"Oh my God!" Aaron cried out, stumbling back from the fallout.

"Get him off me! Get him off me!" she wheezed, sprawling beneath Chuck – his face white behind the helmet's visor, eyes rolled back into his fat head.

Aaron started tugging at the suit of Chuck's arm. He then froze. All the blood was sloshing around inside the helmet, splashing red onto the pale skin. It started seeping from the zipper, onto Amanda's dress.

"Aaron! Come on!" Amanda screeched as she wiggled herself out from under Chuck. The front of her dress was soaked with the red-tinged stain. "Thanks," she snipped, looking down at herself.

Shaking his head, Aaron came out of his daze. He moved to wipe the blood from her dress with his sleeve, but only smeared it worse. Amanda frowned at Aaron's technique, and his hand's proximity to her bosom. He noticed too, then looked down at his feet, and the pool of blood forming a puddle around their shoes.

Like the murky depths of Chuck's blood, the dark gloom surrounded the school as Carl idled past Tremblay's cruiser to park in front of the entrance. "What's going on?" Mike asked from the back seat.

Carl turned to look at him. "I'll just be a minute."

Inside the maintenance room, a broken and limping man, Tremblay, was using the wall for support, after tripping over the spilled sporting equipment. A dented aluminum bat caught his eye, shiny in the dim light. He picked it up, wielding it, before studying the map on the wall again.

With a snort, he felt rejuvenated enough to raise some hell. Staggering from the room, he bashed the bat off a locker door, and started strutting down the hallway, stiff-legged from his knee wound.

"You can't hide in here forever!" he laughed. Some endorphins were kicking in. A manic, menacing grin swept over his crooked face.

Tremblay stopped at the first classroom and poked his head inside for a quick look before continuing on to the next one. "Don't make this worse than it already is!"

The echoing boom of Tremblay's yells resonated inside the library. Aaron and Amanda looked at each other in horror. Immediately, they both turned and started running in the opposite direction, putting as much distance as possible between themselves and the giant who had awoken from his slumber.

Outside the school, Carl dropped a Kevlar vest on the ground, then reached into the open trunk of the cruiser, taking out a 12-gauge short-barrel shotgun. He snagged a few shells out of a box and shoved them in his pocket.

Slamming the trunk closed, Mike watched with a quizzical stare as Carl suited up, in battle armor and weaponry. This was going to be a longer and more serious pit stop than he was led to believe.

Aaron and Amanda rushed past the classrooms, toward the main doors. "What about the money?!" he gasped. "He thinks we still have it. That's why he's chasing us."

Amanda and Aaron slowed to a trot, glancing up the hallway for any sign of movement.

"Where is it?"

"It's in the stairwell."

She nodded. "Okay then, come on..." They continued to the main doors and turned into an adjoining hallway. At the hall, Aaron turned left and Amanda went right. Within a moment, both noticed the other was gone and returned to each other.

"Where are you going?" asked Aaron.

"We need to hide," said Amanda, pulling Aaron to the right with her.

Aaron fought for a moment, digging his heels into the slippery, newly waxed floor. "But we need to get the money first…" Aaron protested weakly before he gave in and followed Amanda.

Not far behind, back at the library, Tremblay squatted beside Chuck's body and pulled a piece of ceiling tile off him.

"Goddamnit, Chuck…"

As Tremblay straightened again, he grimaced at his aching knee pain. Then he noticed something amongst the debris and Chuck's tools. Metallic. Powdered with dust. It was his Colt.

"Son of a bitch." Tremblay picked up the gun, holstered it, and made for the door. Bashing it open with the butt of the baseball bat.

twenty two

Carl slid a shell into the shotgun, walked up to the doors, and then rattled them with all his might. Tremblay heard it, twisted his head round like an owl, wide-eyed and ready to hunt.

Looking down at his cellphone, Carl pressed redial. No answer, just voicemail again. "Jay, what are you doing? Don't do this. I'm at the school. Come outside and we'll talk this over, okay?"

On the other side of the building, Aaron and Amanda wandered into the cafeteria. "But, there's no way out in here. Wouldn't the theatre be better?"

"We can hide in the kitchen and wait for Carl," she said. "There's knives and stuff."

Aaron shook his head, but followed all the same. Still that teacher-student dynamic. Follow Miss Becker, regardless of whether it's a dumb plan.

They hurried past empty tables on the way to the kitchen. It looked like a spooky old ghost town without any children, sitting and eating. Instead of the clatter of cutlery, there was only the sound of their footsteps.

Aaron walked into the serving area and started scouting for weapons.

"I can't believe this is happening," Amanda said, turning to stand guard at the kitchen door, gripping the crowbar so tightly that her knuckles were turning shades of snow.

Looking over, Aaron could see Amanda shaking into a sob. "I'm sorry, Miss Becker…"

"Amanda."

"I'm scared too… Amanda."

"What are we going to do?" she asked, as she lay the crowbar down on a stainless steel counter and rubbed her weary eyes.

"I don't know… But I'm sure not going down without a fight."

Aaron ripped open a cupboard then a drawer, looking for anything that could stab, clobber or maim. A plastic tub in the drawer marked 'Eating Utensils.' He dumped it out on the counter. Knives and forks. All plastic.

Bending the knife between his finger and thumb, he knew they were screwed. "I'm sorry about all this, Miss Beck… Amanda."

"It's not your fault," she said, straining to sound convincing.

"It kind of is though. If I hadn't taken the money, we wouldn't have ended up in this mess."

"You were just doing the right thing though. For your father." Amanda moved to put an arm around Aaron. Partly to comfort him, and partly because she needed a hug, too.

"Yeah, my father. He's an asshole, Amanda," Aaron said, shrugging away from her. "All he cares about is money. Do you know he's not even coming to the play Monday night? After all that bullshit he told me about 'finally seeing me in my element.' He'd rather have another of his stupid meetings. Can you believe it?"

Amanda separated her lips, but had nothing to say. She happened to look up at the glass panels, separating the cafeteria from the hallway; Tremblay was standing there! His hand cupped to the glass, trying to peek inside.

Quickly, she flattened her body against the kitchen wall. "He's here!"

"Oh my God..." Aaron whispered, snatching the crowbar from the counter. "Maybe he didn't see you?"

Then came the sickly sweet tones of Tremblay in, finally, a good mood. "Alright, folks. It's time we wrap this up."

He saw her.

twenty three

Standing by the doors to the gym, Carl pumped the shotgun. With a pair of headlights sweeping behind him, Principal Parker had returned, but was oblivious to Carl, or any other shenanigans inside the school. His school.

Ready, aim, fire. BLAM! Carl dispensed the shell and then kicked the blown apart door open and entered. He racked another shell into the chamber and moved down the shadowy hallway.

Amanda slid down the wall, grabbing tightly onto Aaron's arm. They both huddled down near the ground, as Tremblay's vengeful words hovered over the abandoned cafeteria. "If I have to go in there… it's gonna get messy. So, get your asses out here right now!"

"He's going to kill us," Amanda hissed at Aaron. He looked into her face. Her eyes were beautiful when they were frightened.

"I have an idea," Aaron suddenly said, slicing through the ominous tension.

Tremblay clunked the bat to the floor beside his leg and wiped away the blood caking his left ear. "I'm going to count to…"

"No need." Aaron exited the kitchen holding the crowbar, with Amanda right behind him.

Eyes slitted with suspicion, eyebrows raised with shock; Tremblay looked around the glass partition to see Aaron and Amanda coming out. "Lose the crowbar."

"No."

119

Tremblay raised the bat up into both of his hands and took a large step in their direction. Amanda and Aaron stopped in their tracks. Aaron was dying to swallow, but knew the rise and fall of his Adam's apple would tell Tremblay everything he needed to know: Aaron was nervous.

"I don't suppose you have the money with you?" Tremblay said, scanning them for any bags or perceivable bulges.

Aaron shook his head.

"Of course you don't. Well, let's go get it then."

Aaron looked to Amanda, with an invisible wink. "Ready?" he mumbled.

She sniffed, still fighting back tears. "Don't do this, Aaron. Maybe he'll let us go after..."

Frowning, Aaron looked sternly at Amanda. In a harsh whisper: "We're witnesses, Amanda. He's not going to let us go. This is our only chance."

Tremblay took another large step. It was now or never.

twenty four

"Hey, let me out!"

Principal Parker heard the muffled yell, as he passed by Carl's cruiser outside the school. Then came the soft thud of a thumping fist against glass. Greasy fingerprints smeared together.

Opening the door, Parker frowned and said, "What's going on here, Michael?"

Mike - who was looking ruffled and hot under the collar after being locked in the rear of a cop-car and then losing the cop to a random 'I'll be back' - clambered out and glanced around.

"Those assholes tried to kill me and Aaron and Steve!"

Parker screwed up his face at the curse word, but let it go for the sake of expediency. "What 'assholes'? What are you talking about?"

"The bank robbers! Are Aaron and Steve okay?"

"Aaron? Yes, he's all right."

"Oh, good, they got away," Mike said, sighing as he followed Parker in the direction of the school.

Attempting to glean information from any source, even if it was a boy previously locked inside a car, with seemingly less wherewithal than himself.

Parker asked, "Did that have anything to do with what's going on here?"

"How the heck should I know?" Mike shrugged, his mind onto more pressing things, such as the contents of the school's vending machine.

Neither Parker nor Mike had a clue what was going on, especially at that exact second in the cafeteria…

Aaron knew this was his last chance. Summoning up every ounce of strength and courage, he took a deep breath and did the unthinkable – he charged at Tremblay with a war cry. "Arrrhhhhh!" Crowbar coiled back in his hand, ready to strike.

Although it wouldn't normally be a fair fight – a grizzled Sheriff versus high-school rich kid - it seemed better to die trying, than just die. Still, Tremblay didn't anticipate such guts; maybe they were teaching these kids something in school after all. As a result, he was caught completely by surprise as Aaron swung the bar at him.

Quickly, Tremblay reacted, raising the baseball bat, blocking the crowbar with a clang. Aaron countermoved like a swordsman and poked Tremblay in the ribs. There was a light crack, hopefully he broke a bone. Tremblay grunted and struck back at Aaron with a swipe of the bat, but Aaron was nimble, ducking out of the way. He had the upper hand.

Aaron jousted forward with a mighty thrust, disarming Tremblay. The bat clattered to the ground.

Yet, while holding his aching ribs with his left hand, Tremblay swiftly found the handle of his Colt with his right hand.

Aaron looked back, to see Amanda slinking along the far wall toward the exit. "Run, Amanda!"

Tremblay's gun was released from the holster, its mouth angry and ready to fire. Amanda was suddenly frozen against the wall. Couldn't move another inch. Then, Tremblay aimed towards Aaron.

Running. About to make it. Tremblay squeezed the trigger, blowing apart a glass panel just a few feet in front of Aaron.

Undeterred, Aaron leapt onto a table and jumped – head-first – breaking through the remaining shards of glass, accidentally dropping the crowbar as he rolled to the floor outside the cafeteria.

The tinkling sound of broken glass continued to ring out around him. He looked up, starry eyed, still dazed, but no time to sleep now. He put down his hand and nicked his palm on a sliver. This woke him up. Pain. Don't want any more of that, thank you.

Aaron twisted his body around and rose to his feet. He hustled away from the cafeteria, slipping on the blanket of shards at his feet, before finding enough traction to run down the hallway. Empty-handed. Without the crowbar. Or, Amanda.

"Hey kid! You forgot your girlfriend," Tremblay shouted, echoing down the hall.

Looking back, Amanda tip-toed onto the glass carpet, with a Colt fixed to her temple, Tremblay's hand followed, then his arm, then his cold stare and sneering face. Aaron slowed in front of the main doors. Head spinning. What to do? Go back into the lion's den or get out by the skin of his teeth…

Suddenly, the rattle of doors – Principal Parker with his key in the lock! "What's wrong with this thing?" he mumbled, shaking the jammed door handles. It was the best damn thing Aaron heard all night.

"Help me, help me!" Aaron cried out, rushing to the locked doors.

"Aaron?" Mike said.

"What's going on in there, Aaron? Why is the door locked?"

"The Sheriff locked it. Get help. Get Carl. Hurry!" Aaron cried, abandoning the door, as Tremblay made a beeline for

123

him, with a clump of Amanda's hair anchored to his hand, dragging her along.

Parker scratched his head. "I don't understand. Carl's already here."

But Aaron was gone. With Tremblay hot on his heels.

twenty five

Carl walked out of the library, his eyes struggling to make out shadows of objects and silhouettes in the dim light of the hallway. A flickering exit sign illuminating his path. He turned, hefting the shotgun in both hands, and started down the corridor. Took the next corner, and Aaron ran right into him, his forehead knocking into Carl's chin.

The shotgun fired, accidentally, BLAM! The shrapnel bit a gaping hole in a locker door. Aaron fell backwards, holding his ears, deaf from the blast. "Christ, Aaron, what the hell are you doing? I almost killed you," Carl barked in shock, looking at the torn metal of the locker, and then back to Aaron.

"Oh my God, Carl, I'm so glad to see you," Aaron shouted, unable to hear the true volume of his own voice. "The Sheriff's trying to kill us. He wants the money and he killed Chuck and now he has Amanda and he wants..."

Carl blinked. "He has Amanda? Where is he?"

Thumbing back in the direction from where he came, Carl ran off, as Aaron then wiggled his thumb inside his ear. The elongated tinnitus was slowly getting quieter as volumes returned back to normal.

"Sounds like the cavalry's here, so I don't have much time," hissed Tremblay, still clutching Amanda's hair. They were hiding in her English classroom. He finally released his grip, only to grab hold of the sleeve of her dress – ripping it.

"What are you doing?!" Amanda croaked, trying to back away. Tremblay clung to the fabric, tearing a longer strip off her dress, leaving it shredded on one side – exposing a strip of pale flesh and the hint of a bra strap.

"Get on your knees," he ordered.

Amanda shook her head, until Tremblay cocked the trigger of the Colt, its mouth poised to shoot again.

"You can go now or you can go later," he reminded her.

She got the point, lowering herself to her bruised and scraped knees, unsure of what Tremblay had in mind for her.

"Give me your hands" was his next command. She lifted her palms into the air in front of her. Tremblay holstered his Colt, took her wrists and wrapped the torn fabric around them. He made a knot and then pulled the makeshift cuffs tight with his teeth.

"Maybe we can get Mohammed to come to the mountain," Tremblay whispered in Amanda's ear as she quivered, turning her cheek from his repugnant breath.

Outside in the hallway came Carl's voice: "Sheriff? Where are you?"

Amanda's heart lurched in her chest. Her eyes darted to the door, then back to Tremblay standing over her. "Don't say a word, or I'll kill you now," he whispered sharply.

With a finger to his lips, he hauled Amanda upwards onto her own feet and forced her with him across the room to the windows. Looking down at the heavy iron radiator, Tremblay smiled as he fastened Amanda to it.

"Now stay put," he said.

Carl could feel the shotgun getting heavier and more slippery in his sweaty hands. "Don't hurt her, Jay. Please?" he called out, hoping that Tremblay was close enough to overhear. "She has nothing to do with this."

With dramatic effect, Tremblay side-stepped out of Amanda's classroom, Colt holstered, hands outstretched in front of him, palms up in a 'don't shoot' mime. "We need to talk."

twenty six

Outside, crickets chirping, Principal Parker swallowed a large gulp, upon finding the side entrance to the school was not only unlocked but obliterated. "I think you should wait outside," he murmured to Mike, who wasn't about to let anyone stand in the way of his curiosity.

Mike shoved past Parker and bolted into the darkness of the school.

"Michael! Get back here!" Parker called under his breath, scared he might alert any nearby intruders. Then he glanced over his shoulder, in case of attack from behind, and cautiously entered the school building, unsure of where he would be safer – in or out.

Trying a light switch, Parker made his way to the Maintenance Room, where he saw the smashed electrical boxes. "This is unbelievable... Damn vandals in my school. What is this world coming to?"

Mike knew better. He had found Chuck's bullet-riddled body in the library. This wasn't the work of intruders or vandals. The Pineville Heist was still happening, it wasn't over; the robbers were here to finish the job.

On the other side of the school, in a stairwell, Aaron was snatching the handle to the backpack and scooping up the haul from the robbery. This was the only ticket out of this nightmare, give Tremblay what he wants, in a way that somehow lets him and Amanda escape without so much as a scratch. Try to make some kind of trade that doesn't end with a bullet in each of their backs.

Amanda was thinking of similar things, while strapped to the radiator, a piece of her own dress tied around her mouth as a gag. She pulled as hard as she could, but both the dress fabric and the radiator were holding firm.

"There's nothing to talk about, Jay. Let them go," Carl's voice trailed in from the corridor.

"I can't do that, Carl." Tremblay's voice was direct and booming. The sound of his Colt being drawn, unbridled from the leather holster, friction-free and fast like a gunslinger, and then a single shot – BANG!

Amanda snapped straight, every vertebra in her spine on edge, as she screamed, a wet long agonizing cry into her gag.

The smell of gun smoke drifted into the classroom. It was a dizzying scent and overpowered her other senses. Nothing mattered from this point on. There was no going back. The damage was done. Amanda stopped screaming and surrendered to the gag and the radiator.

Parker heard the gunshot, too. Ran from his office, unsure which direction would guarantee his safety.

Meanwhile, a second shot was looming. Tremblay's boots squeaked as they stepped closer to Carl's body; blood oozing from a bullet hole near his chest. He ripped the shotgun, pried from Carl's cold dead hands, and aimed it. A confirmation round, shoot right to the eye. Carl was lifeless. Not even a twitch. Tremblay changed his mind at the last second, rather than soak his boots in any brain matter, and walked off towards the library.

A trembling Principal Parker practically bumped into Tremblay, right outside the library doors. "Wh-wh-what is going on, Sheriff?" he stammered, intimidated by the shotgun raised to head-level. "Why is Carl shooting up half my school?"

Tremblay nodded slickly. "That's what I'm trying to find out."

"Where are Aaron and Miss Becker? Have you seen Mi--?"

"That little bugger was in on it the whole time," Tremblay said, conniving and scheming with every word.

"What?" Parker said, caught completely off guard by this fresh twist of events.

"The robbery. He was trying to rip his old man off and now look what he's gotten himself into," Tremblay explained, weaving a web of deceit, with Aaron trapped right in the middle. "That boy has been spinning a tale all day long. He's already killed at least two people, including my deputy."

Below their feet, unbeknownst to either of them, Aaron had brought the backpack into the dark confines of the basement, which housed a musty collection of broken black boards, old lockers, filing cabinets and books. Just a single dim bulb suspended from the raftered ceiling. At the very rear, a caged-off section stood a mesh of metal, with an open swing door and a dangling open padlock, containing the majority of the hardback textbooks, stacked on shelves, in rows upon rows, as well as pens, pencils and other supplies. The school's book dispensary.

Aaron glanced at the dusty collection and wondered if Principal Parker knew that the whole lot would easily fit onto his paper-thin iPad device.

Up above him, Amanda was desperately stretching her leg out as far as she could, in an attempt to drag over a desk. Even with her calf muscle at breaking point and her baby toe at its limit, the desk was too far away.

She yelled another muffled scream into her gag in frustration and gave a few more feeble tugs at her restraints.

Amanda knew that even with the adrenaline coursing through her system, she couldn't keep this up all night.

Eventually, it would be curtains for her. She had to think smart, use her last ebbs of energy for maximum effect. Her eyes scanned a room that they had wandered a million times before, during boring show-and-tells, dumb parent-teacher meetings, and bad Shakespearean acting. What had she missed those million times that could help her now?

The window, right beside her! She thought for a second then swung her leg up. Grasping the heel of her shoe in her bound hands, Amanda slipped it off and thwacked it against the glass. Nothing happened. She smacked it again. A slight crack in the glaze. This might just work…

twenty seven

"How could those kids have come up with something like this?" Parker scratched his bulbous head like a pitcher adjusting his jock strap. It was inconceivable to him. Was it because the students at his school were completely dense, or was it because he heard a ring of untruth in the tale?

Tremblay wasn't sure either way, but kept a hawk-like eye on the Principal as he stroked his skull one more time, before giving it a well-earned break.

"I just can't believe they're involved," Parker concluded.

Mike emerged from the library, and he caught a glimpse of Tremblay slowly leveling the shotgun behind Parker's back. His heart skipped a beat.

"Mister Parker!" Mike yelled in a panicked screech.

Spinning around, Parker caught a gut full of lead, blasting him against the library door. He groaned, holding his bleeding stomach together, as he crumpled in a heap on the floor.

With eyes the size of dinner plates, Mike gasped and then back-stepped to retreat, looking to Tremblay and the shotgun being directed at him. But this was it. No escape this time. Click!

Mike winced - but the lead never came. Tremblay had already taken his last shot.

In a flash, a brainwave pulsed down Mike's body to his legs, which burst into movement, carrying Mike off down the hallway. Seemingly possessed by an Olympic sprinter, Mike sped away from Tremblay in a dash for his life.

"Come back, you little shit!" Tremblay hollered, stepped forward, and then opted to turn back and trot in the opposite direction – where he'd left his leverage, tied to a radiator.

Mike's legs lost steam outside the Maintenance Room where he noticed the door to the roof. He pushed the door open and, in another surge, he ran up the stairs...

Entering from another stairwell, Aaron slipped back onto the main level, creeping tightly along the wall. Now it was time to make his deal, now that the cash was stashed where Tremblay wouldn't find it easily.

Aaron glanced out the window – still pitch black outside. All he wanted was to see the dawn, a ray of sunlight at the end of this darkness.

Amanda had pinned her hopes of escape on a dagger of glass that had cracked from the window pane. Bloody from her fumblings - when she had sliced her foot on the sharp glass upon picking it up from the ground and cut her hand when using the makeshift knife -- she managed to cut the fabric enough to tear it. Free at last!

She hobbled to the door on her good foot, where Tremblay had returned and was already bending over Carl's body, pulling a couple of shotgun shells out of his pocket. One fell and rolled under a locker. He loaded the other when he looked up – Amanda started moaning behind her gag, seeing Carl's body for the first time.

Tremblay sighed and raised himself to his feet. "Nice try, missy." He reached for her arm, but she whirled around and slashed Tremblay's hand. A long gash erupted across the back of his knuckles; he dropped the shotgun, howling in pain.

She ran, limping every step of the way. Bloody footprints in her wake. Tremblay bit his lip to suppress the pain, as he snatched the shotgun and aimed it at his fleeing prisoner. She looked back, quickly ducking into the science classroom. A blast of shotgun pellets obliterated the door frame, right where she was standing a moment before.

Aaron glanced down at Parker's body, with a charred and curdled stomach wound; he jogged past. The school was turning into a war zone. Shrapnel and bullet holes, bodies piling up.

Pulling the Colt from his waistband, Aaron thought, 'It's a good thing that I'm armed.'

twenty eight

Desks were thrown asunder as Tremblay barreled through the science classroom towards Amanda, tossing everything that got in his way.

Amanda pulled down the gag from her mouth and maneuvered behind the large lab counter. Bolted down, not going anywhere.

"Please don't! Please..."

"I'm tired of screwing around!" Tremblay growled, reloading another shell into the shotgun.

She needed to do something. Ducking down behind the counter, she flung open the built-in cabinet doors and started looking for a weapon to aid her defense.

Tremblay angled himself around the lab counter, ready to fire, when Amanda popped up – flinging a beaker of clear fluid into his face.

Stunned, Tremblay backed away, the liquid dripping down onto his uniform. He waited for some kind of hideous chemical reaction, where he would begin clawing at his face and screaming in distress as his skin melted and bubbled. Perhaps that's what would've happened if Amanda was a Science teacher and not an English teacher.

Instead Tremblay wiped the water from his nose and his eyes flickered with anger. Amanda squealed staggering backwards into a shelf of vials and beakers. Gun raised, Tremblay clambered over the lab counter, reaching for her. Just as she started throwing everything at him - an eyewash

135

bottle, scale, test tube tray, thermometer, protective goggles - all bouncing off.

Finally, with a deep breath, slightly damp, Tremblay looked steely at Amanda and said, "All done? My turn."

The shotgun lifted to target Amanda as she sobbed.

"Nooooooo!" Aaron yelled, rushing into the lab with the Colt pointed at Tremblay.

Tremblay grinned an all-knowing smile, swinging the shotgun barrel to face Aaron.

CLICK.

Aaron pulled the trigger, but Tremblay didn't collapse with a bullet embedded in his chest. He laughed, tickled by Aaron's confusion, "I'm not stupid enough to fall for that trick twice in a row, kid… Those idiots just needed that one at the bank for show. Now where's my money?"

Aaron stared blankly at the dummy gun. Still shell-shocked, until Tremblay repositioned the shotgun back on Amanda.

"Okay, okay. I'll take you to it."

"Where. Is. It?"

"The basement."

"We're going on a field trip, Miss Becker. Come on – move your ass." Tremblay gestured with the shotgun and followed behind Aaron and Amanda.

Maybe his dad was right. Maybe he'd never amount to nothing. Never be successful like him. Couldn't even shoot a gun when it counted. Or have the smarts to make sure the gun was even loaded.

In the hallway, Amanda whimpered to see Carl, just lying there. "Oh, Carl..."

Tremblay brutishly rammed the shotgun barrel into Aaron's kidney. "Keep moving!"

Aaron released all the air from his lungs, dropping to his knees, keeling over. His cheek slapped against the cool tile floor. It felt reassuring in its chill. Like a shower on a hot summer's day. He felt alive, even though he was so close to death.

"Get up! No more games!"

Amanda reached for Aaron's hand to help him up. As Aaron rose to his feet, he spotted the shotgun shell under the locker.

"Now keep moving…" Tremblay muttered, as Aaron and Amanda continued down the hallway at a snail's pace. With Amanda's injured foot, and Aaron's exhaustion, they were quite a pair. Leaning on each other just to keep walking in a straight line.

Amanda saw Parker's body ahead of them; they had to step around it. "Oh my God… You bastard!" cried Amanda.

"Okay, that's it. I've had enough out of you," Tremblay snapped, adjusting the shotgun in his hands.

"No! Please…" Aaron pleaded.

Wrenching Amanda from Aaron's side, Tremblay took her over to the library door and pushed her inside.

Amanda deflated, realizing this is probably it for her. She gave Aaron a fleeting teary look of goodbye and entered, resigned to her fate. But Tremblay didn't follow behind her. He jammed the shotgun through the dual door handles, barricading her inside.

Turning back to Aaron, unsheathing his Colt, Tremblay signaled with a flick of his wrist that it was just the two of them now. "Let's go."

Behind him, Aaron could hear Amanda, openly weeping.

"I'll tell you right now, kid, if the money's not there, I'm just going to shoot you both and look for it myself."

Aaron nodded. "It's there."

Opening the door to the stairwell, Tremblay leaned over the edge of the railing and glanced down, before following

Aaron into the bowels of the building. "Just out of curiosity, what possessed you to take my money in the first place?"

"It's not yours," Aaron said surely, as he turned the handle, opening the next door into the basement. Stale air wafted into their faces. They entered.

"The hell it ain't," Tremblay said, getting his britches in a knot. "Do you have any idea how much bullshit I've had to take from people like your father who thinks I'm just some sort of glorified slave whose only job it is to kiss his ass while he sells us all down the river?"

Aaron glanced over his shoulder briefly, leading Tremblay past the old lockers and black boards, stopping a few feet from the open cage door. He looked over to Tremblay, making eye contact, trying to read his next move. "Before I tell you where it is, will you promise me one thing?" Aaron asked. "Will you let Miss Becker go? I'm sure if you gave her some of the money she wouldn't say anything and..."

Tremblay's eyes trailed away from Aaron's; he noticed something on the floor behind Aaron. A $100 bill... and behind that by the cage door is another. He doesn't need this stupid kid any more. "The only thing I'm going to promise is to make sure they spell your names right in the obit--"

Just like Aaron thought – he dived behind a stack of filing cabinets as Tremblay fired. A ricocheting bullet bounced off the cabinets and disappeared, like Aaron, into the basement's shadows.

Then, silence. Tremblay aimed into the dark and pulled the trigger – it disappeared like the other - but that was his last bullet.

CLICK. Empty.

twenty nine

The trap was set. A $100 bill was the cheese, attracting the rat towards the cage.

Tremblay narrowed his eyes and crinkled his nose. Then he saw the rest of the loot, just resting on the table, the bulging backpack. He rushed into the caged area of the basement and scrambled over to the table, like an amorous lover about to embrace a much-missed beau at the airport.

The teeth of the zipper unpeeled in a second and Tremblay was confronted with something worse than stinking cheese – a stack of dusty textbooks. And he just fell for the oldest trick in one of them. A case of bait and switch.

The cage door clanged shut behind him and the seething face of Tremblay flicked around to see Aaron clicking the padlock shut through the door's slot. Locked in.

Foam bubbling at his lips, Tremblay leapt forward with a guttural inhuman roar. He lashed out but couldn't reach Aaron, who hopped backwards, admiring his catch.

"You're dead, you little bastard!"

Aaron exhaled and leaned against a filing cabinet, slowly feeling the tension leaving his body. Immediately his aching muscles spoke up, reminding him of the day and night that he had just survived. Nevertheless, these were good signs of normality returning. The nightmare was finally over.

Then, feeling an awkward weight pressing into his back, Aaron shifted and pulled the Colt from his pants. He then looked up; Tremblay was fiercely yanking books and school supplies off shelves in a crazed fury. It was amazing, Aaron thought, how even tame beasts become wild when suddenly confined. Freedom was a precious thing, and denying it would be the best punishment for someone like Tremblay. Or would it…

"I wish this thing was loaded so I could blow your head off," Aaron said, surprising himself as he actually meant it.

Tremblay glanced down at the pile of books at his feet. Then his eyes rose to meet Aaron's. It was unnerving, even when Aaron knew he was safe and Tremblay was a caged man.

"Can I have it back?" Tremblay said.

Aaron frowned, thoughtfully examining the gun in his hand. "Why?" Then his eyes widened, the bigger picture dawning on him. "Oh my God. This is the gun you were looking for, isn't it? At the campsite, just before you killed that guy - you were asking about a gun..." Aaron smirked to himself. "You lent your own cowboy gun to the other bank robbers! What a doofus."

Slamming against the bars, Tremblay grabbed the metal door and shook it with all his might. But, Aaron felt superior by this point. He stood his ground. Kicked the cage. Laughed for the first time in what felt like weeks, when it had only really been hours since he, Steve and Mike had shared a laugh on their walk to the forest… Not so long ago.

"I'm not scared of you anymore. As soon as the police get here, you're going to get what you deserve."

Tremblay tapped his badge with authority. "You're forgetting something, I am the police."

"Nah, I'm talking about the ones Mike called by now… So, you can just find a comfy spot over in the corner and wait for the <u>real</u> cops to arrive."

It was only a split second, but Aaron had stepped too close to the claws of a predator. Tremblay lurched at the cage, reaching as far as his arm could've allowed, clutching a handful of Aaron's shirt collar.

Pulling it tight, Tremblay had him. Didn't matter on what side of the bars you were on, if one of you's dead and one of you's alive. There's only one winner in those circumstances.

A sharp gasp, Aaron struggled to move and then realized he had bigger problems, as he struggled to breathe. Tremblay drew the shirt collar in with his white-knuckled fist, cutting off Aaron's air.

Water filled in Aaron's eyes, blurring the room into shady blobs and smears. He flailed his arms, reaching for the edges of the cage, coughing out the choke in his throat.

"I told you I was going to kill you first chance I got." The words were far away, fading into the recesses of the disappearing basement.

Then, Aaron felt something prickly and sharp at his fingertips that awoke his mind, jolting him back to reality – the rough grip of the Colt, as he pulled it from his waistband.

"What are you going to do with...?" Tremblay grunted as he received an abrupt answer to his question – the gun's barrel speared sharply into Tremblay's crotch, doubling him over in pain, and he immediately released Aaron's collar.

Tremblay fell backwards and Aaron tumbled the other way, choking and sputtering. Aaron rubbed his throat and Tremblay softly patted his jewels; the two stared at each other with a momentary respect - like two warriors acknowledging each other's strength in battle.

This wasn't over. Tremblay would never quit. Aaron could see it burning in his foe's eyes. Tremblay placed his hand on a shelf, easing himself up, and then suddenly he ripped the plank from its ledge. Aaron blinked as Tremblay rushed back to the cage door and started hammering the plank on top of the lock with a brute force. And then again. And again. And again. A small dent appearing in the lock's metal edging.

Aaron realized exactly what Tremblay was doing. He pulled himself up, still catching his breath, and he dashed for the exit. Not looking back. Leaving behind the sound of a beast trying to break free from its cage.

thirty

Mike looked up at the dark night's sky. A blanket of stars, the hue of Venus perhaps too. Well, maybe it was Venus. He never could tell whether it was a planet or just another star.

He sighed to himself and glanced to the only door on the rooftop – no handle on the outside. He wasn't going anywhere. Plenty of time to debate if that bright dot was really a star, a planet, or a motorcycle headlight in some faraway galaxy.

Amanda was heading upwards, too. She had scouted around the library, trapped like Mike and Tremblay, and decided to ascend the ladder into Chuck's domain; the ceiling. Dark and dangerously dusty with asbestos and God only knows what else.

She crawled forwards, holding her breath with cutely pursed lips, as the ceiling tiles heaved under the weight of her knees and elbows.

Little cracks were appearing, sending crumbling white matter down from the rafters, like confetti on the typewriter-lined desks of a business classroom below. Just as Aaron ran by, reaching the library doors, and pulling the shotgun free of the handles, tossing it aside. But, Amanda was already gone, moving stealthily above him.

"Amanda? Miss Becker?" Aaron hissed, glancing around the quiet room. As quiet as a library in fact. "It's okay, you can come out..."

His mind was ticking over time, and then he saw the ladder and his pupils walked up the steps into the hole in the ceiling. Aaron clambered up, following the path created in his thoughts, and looked inside.

"Amanda! Come back! It's okay… I locked him up," the word echoed into the opening.

He heard a shuffle and a muffled voice. Amanda was turning around. She was coming back.

Maybe this was all going to work out.

But, Tremblay had other plans; he smiled at the broken lock on the ground in front of the caged door. He was slightly taken aback at his own success. Snapping out of his daze, he discarded the wood shelf in his hands.

Tremblay strolled out of the cage, stopping to pick up the 'bait', the $100 bill. He deposited it in his pocket and then hastened out of the basement, the wicked glint of payback in his beady eyes.

thirty one

Amanda's face slowly emerged out of the darkness. Aaron smiled and she smiled back at him. "Really, he's trapped?"

"Yeah, yeah. I tricked him. Come on out of there," Aaron said, dipping back into the library.

Slowly but surely, she continued crawling to the light that was coming from the hole in the ceiling. Aaron descended the ladder with a smile. It was a short-lived one. Wiped from his face, as the library doors slammed open, and Tremblay charged inside.

"Nooooooo!" Aaron screamed out. Amanda knew all too well what was happening. Only one man could have such an effect on Aaron's vocal chords. A doggedly determined sheriff looking for his bag of stolen money.

Thinking fast, Aaron gripped the sides of the ladder and rushed up the steps, two at a time, pulling himself up into the hole. Still holding the ladder, Aaron twisted around and hoisted it up with him, just out of Tremblay's clawing grasp!

A baseball bat clenched in his hands, Tremblay hurled the weapon at Aaron, missing again, and bouncing off a ceiling joist before falling back down to the floor.

Tremblay could only watch feebly as Aaron slid the remaining half of the ladder into the hole. Gone.

"Nice trick kid... but it's not over!" Tremblay barked, picking up the fallen baseball bat.

As Aaron crawled off into the blackness of the ceiling, guided only by thin shafts of light leaking around the edges of

145

the tiles; Tremblay walked along beneath him, monitoring the bangs and bumps.

There was a flash of movement in the shadows up ahead; Amanda hadn't got far. "Hurry, he's coming," Aaron urged her.

"I thought you said he…"

"He got out, okay? Go, go, go!"

They scrambled across 10 feet of ceiling, but it felt like 20 or 30, with scraped stinging knee caps and bruised knuckles. Then, Aaron slowed to a halt. Amanda heard him stop and turned around. "What is it, Aaron?"

"Nothing, that's just it… If he was coming, we'd hear him."

Amanda screwed up her face and strained to hear a noise, any noise, but Aaron was right. Silence. Unsettling, eerie, emptiness.

WUMP! Until the baseball bat exploded through the ceiling tile, right in front of Amanda! She screamed rolling to one side, as the bat pierced another gaping hole to the left of her.

Below, Aaron could see the menacing snarl of Tremblay standing atop a desk in the business classroom, aiming the bat for another poke at them.

"Move, move, move!" Aaron implored as the bat protruded between his legs, a narrow miss. No time for niceties now, Aaron gave Amanda's butt a hefty shove to keep her moving.

Then, Tremblay had a direct hit – breaking through the tile right underneath Aaron, stabbing the baseball bat's tip into his stomach with a jolt. Aaron grunted but kept crawling. There would be worse than that if Tremblay actually got his hands on him and Amanda.

Tremblay followed the dips in the ceiling and hopped to the next desk, heaving the bat up into another ceiling tile, knocking it upwards and off kilter.

"It's just a matter of time, people," he wheezed, stepping to the next desk like a frog hopping lily pads, trying to catch flies.

Then, Tremblay boldly leapt down from the desk; his ears picking up a dull thud near the wall, above the door frame. He zeroed in.

"He's going to get us, Aaron," Amanda coughed, a piece of ceiling shrapnel irritating the back of her throat.

"Stop for a sec," Aaron whispered. "You have to go back."

"What?"

Aaron quickly placed his finger to his lips and looked at Amanda. Again, that silence. Nothing good comes of it.

"He'll never expect us to split up," Aaron told her.

"No, no, no..." She was already shaking her head at the thought of being alone in the darkness of the ceiling, with a mad man on their trail.

"It's our only chance. I'll distract him long enough for you to go back to the library and try to find a way out," Aaron said, trying to convince Amanda, tears welling in her big blue eyes. "Trust me."

Suddenly, another tile exploded up behind them. Tremblay had missed the mark. Amanda stifled a shriek and nodded to Aaron. There was no time to argue. They couldn't play these games all night.

"Don't move until you hear the shit hit the fan, okay?"

Amanda nodded.

"Now lie down flat."

Aaron slowly crawled over the top of Amanda, dragging himself over her to get to the other side. It could almost be considered sensual – body to body, in the warm darkness of the ceiling cavity, nerves jangling, hearts racing, rubbing, an electric friction crackling between their clothing – if it were not for the baseball bat-wielding Sheriff Tremblay, waiting to whack them. What a mood-killer.

With a sigh, Aaron looked at Amanda, one last time. Then lifted the corner of a tile, to peer inside Principal Parker's empty office...

thirty two

Tremblay was poised, standing atop the switchboard desk, with the baseball bat about to jab upwards. Then he heard the thud of movement inside Parker's office, right next door. He smiled a wily grin, and gripped the bat with both hands.

Time to knock that little punk's block off, he thought. Even if it meant never finding the stashed cash, Tremblay was too incensed to care about locating money at that exact second. He just wanted to teach Aaron a lesson he'd never forget. He screwed with the wrong cop. First in the canteen and then in the basement. Now this was his third strike…

Tremblay prepared the bat for a swing, easing into Principal Parker's office. Then in a stealthy stride, he crossed the room, stepped up onto a chair, onto Parker's desk, and rammed the bat skywards.

A ceiling tile lifted off its joist and tumbled to the floor, catching Tremblay's eye as he followed it down, cracking in half on the armrest of the chair.

He took his eye off the prize. Out of nowhere, Aaron's feet careened into Tremblay's skull. The force sent Tremblay into a somersault forwards off the desk, landing awkwardly as the chair broke his fall, and almost his back with it.

With the momentum, Aaron leapt across the gap between tiles. He was short, and his chest slammed into the edge. *Damnit.* His nails scratched for a good grip, his legs dangling.

Like a pair of jeans on a breezy clothes line, he looked down at his flapping limbs.

Hands slipping. Need to throw a knee up, and pull hard. Some diversion he turned out to be. Aaron was meant to throw Tremblay a bone to distract him. Instead he'd thrown him the whole three-course meal! Unless he could just get some leverage. Energy was in short supply at this point. Gravity was stronger than his will, it seemed. He didn't need Tremblay to yank on his ankle, he already felt like weights were tied to his toes.

Then, it got worse. Aaron winced and wailed. The heavy echo of the baseball bat hitting his thigh followed by a shooting pain.

Suddenly, a burst of panic coursed through him, animating his legs into a wild thrashing motion, kicking anything within reach, and creating some distance. Then the bat rammed into his ribs. He was a piñata up there, taking hit after hit.

The sound of the bat being tossed to the ground was unnerving. Tremblay didn't need it anymore. Aaron felt the large paws around his calves, tugging at him.

Half in, half out of the ceiling, Aaron struggled to hang on. Yet, the splintering ceiling tile had the final say in the matter, when it broke into a large section - with Aaron still attached.

A crumbling mass of tile and Aaron collapsed onto the desk. Aaron felt like something soft broke the fall - it was Tremblay, and Aaron was right on top of him.

thirty three

Easing the ladder over the edge of the hole, Amanda slowly extended the frame and then lowered it safely to touch the library floor. Back in this damn library, she thought, looking around at the mess. It was like a never-ending hell and you were caught in quicksand, which kept bringing you back to where you started.

Amanda stepped down and found her footing on the ground. Shaky. Too much time crawling in enclosed spaces. Her knees were shot from all the scraping around. She hobbled on her cut foot to the library doors and effortlessly pushed them open.

A Glock was pointed right at her face. Amanda released a silent scream; her voice was battered, too. Nothing left even for a real fright.

The hand behind the gun was trembling. Carl took aim before he realized it was Amanda.

"Carl…" Amanda stammered, finding it hard to say the words.

She looked down at his shirt, which was half-unbuttoned, revealing his trusty Kevlar vest. Carl slowly lowered the gun, fighting every instinct to keep it raised and shoot anything that moves.

They stepped back inside the library, Amanda wrapping her arms around him and crying. Carl was still sore and quick to push Amanda to arm's length. He rubbed the spot where Tremblay shot him. Felt like his ribs were cracked, it was so bruised.

Amanda sniffed back more tears. "I thought you were…"

"Lucky for me he can't shoot worth a shit with that Colt," Carl said with the gallantry of a Clint Eastwood cowboy after surviving a showdown at high noon.

Tenderly stepping closer, entering Carl's space, Amanda placed her hand on his chest, touching the empty circle - the bullet hole in Carl's shirt. Such a tiny hole, and yet it could've caused so much carnage if not for the vest's protection.

"It is over your heart," she noted.

Carl was too distracted to pick up on any romantic or karmic connotations of a shot to the heart. He looked past her weepy face and directly to the mess behind her. "Where is he?"

"He's chasing Aaron. You have to go after him, Carl."

Carl swallowed deeply as he realized it, too.

thirty four

Tremblay might've cushioned the fall, but he wouldn't want to be a mattress forever. Aaron rolled off, debris sprinkled all over them.

The sleeping giant started to awake, only winded from taking the full brunt of the ceiling collapse, and the weight of a young man tumbling out of the air.

No time to stop and stare, Aaron bolted out of the office and down the corridor. He patted himself as he ran, checking for cuts and broken bones. Thank God, Tremblay was standing where he was. Otherwise, Aaron would be concussed and counting fingers.

Then, he heard the sounds of ceiling tiles cracking on the floor, brushed off of Tremblay as he bristled through the door. The footsteps were loud and stomping, getting faster. Well, as fast as you could be in the condition of the two injured parties.

Aaron felt his legs creaking and jarring with every hobbling movement, after receiving a pounding from Tremblay's bat. Meanwhile, Tremblay had taken a few knocks himself – Amanda's crack to his shin with the crowbar remained excruciating every time he placed weight on his leg. But, both had too much to lose if either stood still to lick their wounds.

Regardless, the ongoing chase had a molasses-like quality to it; as if caught in slow-motion. Yet, despite the lack of speed, Aaron chanced to look back and could already see Tremblay gaining on him, with the baseball bat wielded in his hand, and an intermittent grimace following every other step.

Aaron shuddered as he continued to run in a skip-hop, but nerves were about to get the better of him. He couldn't keep up with this pace. Soon he was gonna get caught. OK, any second now.

The broken glass---seemingly sprinkled like sparkling ice across the floor outside the cafeteria. Aaron skated over it, and lost his footing this time. One hand went down to steady himself, getting sliced with a shard. "Oww... shit!"

He pulled the blood-stained piece of glass from his palm and dropped it, leaving it behind in his dust. He didn't even notice the small trail of red droplets, following his every step. Had to keep going. Find a way out.

Aaron looked towards the door of the school's theatre and slowed from a broken trot to a walk. The poster pinned to the wall seemed to be watching him – his own eyes staring back at him. 'Hamlet'. Aaron was photographed in a period costume holding a sword, like a true Shakespearean thespian. To die or not to die -- that is the question.

With no other options, Aaron shouldered the door and ventured inside. A backstage emergency light was the only illumination in the cavernous auditorium. Aaron wandered towards it, down the aisle between rows and rows of seating.

His eyes were fixed on the stage. His stage. He was meant to be performing up there. All eyes were on him.

He scanned the several pieces of Hamlet scenery, dotted around the stage, in mid-construction practically ready for opening night. If ever there was going to be an opening night.

Aaron hopped up onto the stage, moving past a giant card-board strawberry, and then bumping into a huge wooden cloud, beside a rack of costumes, props and an old toolbox.

It was eerie up there - with the emergency lights glowing across the stage. He was alone. No other actors. No directors. No audience. Just him.

But it wouldn't be for long. Tremblay easily picked up Aaron's trail of blood, leading from the broken glass by the canteen, neatly spaced every two feet or so, all the way to the theatre.

The door was slightly ajar. Tremblay squeezed the handle of the baseball bat and stepped into the theatre, his pupils slowly adjusting to the low light. His mind was racing. If the rest of the night was anything to go by, this kid wouldn't go down without a fight. There might still be some scrap left in him, so Tremblay promised himself that he'd strike first and strike hard.

Too late, the sword blade sliced across Tremblay's cheek! Aaron had dealt the first blow, jumping from the shadows. Tremblay caught off guard, howled, dropping the bat to clutch his face.

Aaron followed up with a nick to the back of Tremblay's leg, effortlessly swinging the sword through the air. Tremblay buckled down to one knee. With no mercy, Aaron dived in for a cut to the gut, but Tremblay opened his hands and fearlessly grabbed the edges of the sword, pulling it from Aaron's grasp.

Holding it up, with bloody hands, Tremblay's expression was grim. "You're dead, kid."

"You won't get away with this," Aaron sputtered, retreating backwards.

Tremblay lifted himself up, with a sneer and the sword. "I already am."

.

thirty five

Dead. Done. Doomed. It was curtains for Aaron. He thought it was ironic that he would die on the stage – something that he'd worried about doing for months. That was, die because his acting was so bad. Not because he was run through with his own sword. How's that for a Shakespearean tragedy?

Nevertheless, tempting fate, Aaron clambered onto the stage, not taking his eyes away from Tremblay and the glistening weapon. Aaron backed up, brushing past the strawberry cut-out, as Tremblay stepped onto the stage to join him.

"How are you going to explain all the bodies? All the evidence?" Aaron spat at Tremblay. His words were the only hurdles between himself and that sword, but he used them effectively, like a dying man's last words.

"I don't have to..." Tremblay retorted, as Aaron frowned, genuinely puzzled. "You see, Officer Carl Edward Smith had been planning to rob the bank for months. And it really was a flawless plan, too... I mean to set it all up, watch it go down, then as he was investigating the very crime itself, eliminate all the evidence that leads directly to him and walk away with the money - scot free."

Aaron pointed an accusing finger. "You're going to blame this all on Carl? That's rich."

"About five million dollars rich," Tremblay said, a line of

blood trickling down his cheek from the scratch Aaron inflicted on him.

Aaron was running out of stage, as he moved past the cloud-shaped structure, noticing the rack of props out of the corner of his eye. "You don't have to do this."

"Oh, but I do." Tremblay slashed the air to get a feel for the sword. It felt good.

"I'll bring you to the money."

"I don't care anymore," Tremblay said with a brazen shake of his head. "There's still half of it out at the campsite somewhere."

Aaron suddenly tensed. His bargaining chip had evaporated right in front of him. Tremblay didn't need him. Not alive anyway. It would be daylight soon, and Tremblay was tying up loose ends. And, Aaron was as loose as they come.

A slicing flash was coming Aaron's way, and he quickly ducked down behind the giant cloud and put his hand on another sword. Swinging around, just in time to fend off Tremblay's powerful jab; there was a tremendous clash of metal on metal.

Meanwhile, Carl and Amanda made their way to the main doors. Carl retrieved his handcuff key and unlocked the manacles holding the door posts sealed. One tiny key solved all those major headaches with a single twist. He pushed open a door for Amanda. "I'll be out as soon as I…"

Amanda interrupted him with a look that said much more than her question: "But, what if…?"

"You know what to do 'if,'" Carl said firmly, staring fixedly into her eyes.

With a final teary glance, she exited the building. Carl waited a second, checked the ammo clip of his Glock, and went searching for the only two people left in the school. It was doubtful that he would've ever guessed what they were doing at this exact moment.

thirty six

After the Colts and shotguns, now it was all coming down to a sword fight - an old-fashioned duel.

Tremblay made a thrust, Aaron parried. Tremblay slashed wildly, Aaron blocked it with ease. His basic training was paying off. Tremblay kicked Aaron's leg. Aaron faltered a step, though able to dodge a swipe, he was still open – enough to allow Tremblay to easily slice his upper thigh!

His jeans were shredded, and not in a fashionable way, and then the red puncturing of his skin was evidence of Tremblay's perfect cut. Aaron cried out, but didn't let it paralyze him. He kept battling on, retaliating with an upward blow, which Tremblay barely deflected.

Tremblay grunted, he was stronger and gaining the upper hand. Now with their swords' connected in mid-air, Tremblay could maneuver this party wherever he wanted. Aaron's eyes widened as Tremblay forced him backwards into the giant strawberry; knocking it and Aaron over...

Aaron and the two-dimensional shape clattered flat onto the stage, but Aaron was quick to curl his body into a roll and get out of the line of fire. The roll worked, giving way for less surface area for Tremblay to stab at. A few hacks and slashes, narrowly missed him. And then the edge of the stage appeared soon enough, sending Aaron off into the darkness below.

Tremblay hesitated for a second, before leaping after Aaron – but, it was too late when he realized that he should have looked first. Aaron popped up from the inky shadows, holding his sword in front of him; rigid and strong. His heels dug into the theatre's carpeting, ready for the dead weight of a full grown man on the end of his blade.

With the whites of his eyes shining iridescently in fear of the impending impaling, Tremblay veered to the right, tilting his body at the last second to avoid his fate – still, Aaron's sword pierced into his stomach. *Got him.*

The flesh was tough, but the sword was sharp enough with Tremblay's velocity to penetrate – sending him into a high-pitched squeal like a stuck pig. Despite his efforts, Aaron couldn't stop the rest of Tremblay's hefty body from pile-driving into him. Simultaneously, bashing the sword and Aaron in different directions, both falling to rest on the ground.

Aaron looked to his left. His sword lying out of reach be-hind Tremblay's lifeless corpse. But, he had to be sure. He wouldn't trust this animal that'd escaped a cage and now seemed docile, suffering from an apparently fatal wound.

Clambering to his feet and limping in the direction of the sword, Aaron carefully stepped over Tremblay and edged towards the sword. But, before he could pick it up, Aaron heard a shuffle. He shuddered and clocked his head around to Tremblay – who was alive and scraping himself along, blood spilling from the gash in his gut!

"Come here you little bastard!" Tremblay lashed out with his words, and his madly flailing arms, still clinging to his own sword.

Dodging the swings, Aaron stepped onto the nearest seat, just as the seat next to him ripped open, foam billowing out. Then the following swipe was right on target, smacking the broad side of the sword against the backs of both Aaron's legs – buckling him backwards into the welcoming arms of his nemesis.

Tremblay swept up his prize, taking a clump of Aaron's hair into his fist. His hot, foul breath was inches from Aaron's ear. "How'd you like that?!"

"Ow, ow, ow..." Aaron grumbled, feeling his hair being tugged back to the stage.

This wasn't how he planned it. This wasn't what he wanted. But, this wasn't like in rehearsals. This was real life. And this script was about to get a new ending, written by Tremblay – the sword was mightier than the pen, in this case.

Feeling any speck of hope drifting out of his grasp, Aaron suddenly fought back from the brink of giving up. He put his hand down and grabbed Tremblay's Achilles' heel – his bleeding gut – and squeezed the wet mess of intestines and muscle.

It was literally a gut-wrenching twist. Tremblay didn't know whether to scream, cry or die. He immediately dropped Aaron's hair and turned pale from the sheer agony.

Seizing the momentary lapse, Aaron didn't waste a single second. He broke away from Tremblay, raced for the stage, jumped up, and beat a path towards the cloud scenery.

However, the torturous pain in his abdomen only enraged Tremblay and he poured every ounce of his anger into a mad dash after Aaron, following him onto the stage, charging at him.

Then, the two found themselves evenly matched again, with Aaron grabbing another sword off the props pile in the nick of time. "You still want to play, huh?" Tremblay growled through gnashed teeth.

Aaron only looked guiltily at his sword and then back at Tremblay. Filled with fury, and the fearlessness of a man losing blood, Tremblay lashed out – his sword hitting Aaron's leg wound from before, opening it even wider. Aaron gasped.

163

Then he saw Tremblay swing down on his left arm - another vicious cut.

In a daze, suddenly losing blood himself, Aaron staggered in a half-circle. Tremblay mirrored his prey, side-stepping around Aaron, sensing a victory in the making.

Limping meekly, Aaron looked broken and ready for his death knell. Tremblay was all too happy to ring that bell.

When suddenly Aaron tossed his sword at Tremblay's sword hand. A last feeble attempt to chop Tremblay's wrist, or so Tremblay presumed, dropping his own sword in a heart-beat and deftly catching Aaron's thrown sword.

"What do you call that move?" Tremblay scoffed, as Aaron bent down to retrieve Tremblay's dropped weapon, re-arming himself. "Swapsies?"

A spark appeared in Aaron's eyes. The tables had turned again, only Tremblay didn't know it yet. Aaron launched himself at Tremblay who raised the sword in his hand, connecting with the sword now in Aaron's hand – one was a 'replica', a fake, nothing more than a prop. Torn to pieces by the real sword – which was now in Aaron's hand.

Tremblay looked down at the wiggling blade, protruding from his chest, piercing all the way through to the cloud behind him. He was pinned to the set-piece.

"Game over," Aaron said, staggering away from Tremblay who was grinning eerily. Bloody bubbles formed at his mouth. Before slumping dead, hanging from the cloud.

thirty seven

Aaron turned around, hearing the click of the Glock – Carl had entered the theatre, hearing the uproar, and was ready to fire. "Wait! Don't shoot!" Aaron cried out, raising his hands.

Carl's eyes adjusted to the dim light, and then attempted to process the scene in front of him. "Holy shit," he murmured.

"That's what I say," Aaron nodded, walking up the aisle, approaching Carl.

"Let's get out of here," Carl said, lowering his Glock.

"Did Amanda get out okay?"

"Yeah, she's out in the car."

Carl opened the theatre doors, wincing at the pain of his own wounds, before seeing Aaron's cuts in a new light and raising an eyebrow.

"I can't believe all this happened just for that stupid money," Aaron muttered under his breath.

With a nod, Carl sighed nonchalantly. "Did you ever have it?"

"It's in the basement," Aaron said, seeing the main doors ahead of them. A sight he didn't expect to see again. And when they reached them, the cold handle of the door felt very good in his hand.

But, Carl stopped him in his tracks. "We should go get it."

"Now?" Aaron glanced over his shoulder, and then back at the exit he longed for.

"We can't just leave it sitting around. Come on..." Carl ushered Aaron back down the hallway. The familiar squeaks of his shoes in the corridor were a haunting reminder that he'd

165

been down this path before, and all Aaron wanted to do was walk backwards. Pretend this night never happened.

There were signs of violence everywhere they looked. Aaron stepped casually over the strewn shotgun, as he glanced at the library doors on his way past.

"I'm going to make sure you get a reward for this. Amanda, too."

Aaron shrugged. "So, how did you get in?"

"What?"

"The doors were locked."

"I blew off the side door."

"You mean we could have gotten out?" Aaron pondered aloud.

"Lucky for me you didn't," Carl chimed in, to which Aaron shot him a bemused glare. "I mean if you had, then Tremblay would still be out there running around like a maniac," Carl concluded his thought.

"It's here," Aaron said, pointing to the basement door. They followed the stairs down and into the darkened bowels, where Aaron guided Carl to a dented locker. It wasn't even locked. He pulled it open, revealing all the cash from the backpack. Like a vault at Fort Knox, packed from top to bottom.

Carl whistled as he stared at it. "Now that's a lot of money."

Blood money, Aaron thought to himself, as Carl looked left and right, scanning the basement area.

"Find me something to carry it in," Carl nudged Aaron. Despite his injuries, Aaron obeyed the authority figure and started wandering into the darker recesses of the room.

Leaning forward, Carl placed his hand on the top stack of dollar bills. Grabbed it between his fingers and thumbed it. Not enough. Need to smell this small fortune. He took the stack and lifted it to his nose, taking a long sniff, like he was admiring the exquisite bouquet of a fine wine; except he was a connoisseur of money.

"How's this?" Aaron asked, holding up a large text books' box. Carl showed his agreement by tossing the stack of cash to Aaron.

"Do you mind?"

Aaron shook his weary head, catching the stack directly in the box, and wandered back to the locker. Carl smiled and Aaron began scooping the rest of the locker's contents, which tumbled out in a heaping pileful of stacked notes.

"That was pretty smart hiding it," Carl said, watching the mountain of green that was building in the bottom of the box. He fumbled in his pocket for a lollipop. "No wonder Tremblay went ape shit."

Carl's fingers fiddled with the lollipop paper, looking down as he unwrapped the head – creating a distinctive crinkle.

Aaron blanched, slowly shifting his gaze from the locker to Carl's lollipop. It all came flooding back in an instant; he found himself transplanted from the dark basement to the bright woodland scene where he witnessed the bearded man begging for his life, right before his murder in cold blood.

Tremblay aimed the gun as he questioned Jake.
"Gordie's lying," Jake pleaded.
Then, that strange crinkling sound – Aaron had heard it right then, as Carl unpeeled a lollipop and stuck it into his mouth.

He was there! Carl was at the scene of the crime, with Tremblay. They were working together.

"I think you are the one who's lying, amigo," said Tremblay icily.

167

"Please, no, wait. Ask him again."

"I wish I could, but he's..." BLAM!

Tremblay looked back at Carl in surprise, to see Carl slowly lowering his Glock, with a thin line of gunsmoke rising from the muzzle.

Jake collapsed in a heap, inches away from Aaron's face, as he hid beneath the canoe...

"Almost done?" Carl asked, taking the lollipop from his lips.

BLAM! The fatal second shot rang out.

Aaron jumped inside but nodded silently, processing the shifting sands of this new reality. His heart pounded away just as it did under the canoe. He continued to load the last stacks of cash into the box, carefully spying Carl's holstered Glock.

"Okay, buddy. Let's go."

Forcing a smile, Aaron picked up one end of the box and helped Carl carry *his* blood money.

thirty eight

Up the steps, ascending out of the basement, one by one, watching Carl's back, and his still holstered Glock. But, for how long. A loose end for Tremblay was still a loose end for Carl.

Reaching the top of the basement stairs, Aaron inhaled a deep breath. "Why do you think he did it?" he said quickly.

"You should know why. With your old man closing the mill, Pineville will be a ghost town by Christmas."

"So, killing everybody was just part of your twisted retirement party?"

Before he could think, Carl retorted defensively, "We didn't plan on killing anyone. It just…" He suddenly realized what Aaron was asking, and moreover how he had just let the cat out of the bag.

Carl spun around then, as he heard Aaron's end of the box drop and hit the ground. Aaron was running again. Scrambling to release his Glock from the holster, Carl gave chase.

"Get back here!" he shouted, yanking the Glock out into a shooting position, firing off a couple of rounds at Aaron's fleeing form.

Hearing those rogue bullets ricocheting off the floors and walls around him, Aaron couldn't round the corner fast enough. He sucked in everything, hoping to make a narrow target, and veered to the right – out of Carl's line of sight.

This sudden burst of strenuous exercise caused Aaron's leg to start bleeding fresh blood. He slapped a hand over the damp wound, but hobbled on. Then he saw something up ahead – the shotgun.

Just enough time to scoop up the weapon and keep moving. He bent down, snatched up the shotgun, and heard the next shot from Carl's Glock. The bullet sailed overhead.

The English class was getting close. Aaron's mind was counting the imaginary steps that he needed to make to reach the classroom door. Too many.

With another snap of gunfire, Aaron blinked. Toppling over, skidding to a halt on the polished floor. He was down.

Staying close to the wall of lockers, Carl trained his Glock on Aaron's body. After this night, he was ready for anything. So he thought.

Carl licked his upper lip, a bead of sweat rolling down from his nose. Finger hovered over the trigger. Then, Aaron slowly rolled over, holding the shotgun with one hand and his other hand clenched in a fist.

"Don't move!" Carl screeched, tensing at the sight of the shotgun. But, he recognized it as his shotgun – relaxing immediately, as he knew it was empty. This kid played his last card. It was a good one. But, couldn't beat his hand.

Carl sighed. "Look, Aaron - I'm sorry it has to come down to this. But, you really left me no choice here."

Not moving an inch, Aaron simply opened his mouth and asked, "Why, Carl, why?"

"I told you. Because your father is going to sell the mill and…"

"He's investing in it."

"What?" Carl said, letting go of the Glock's grip with his other hand to scratch the back of his head.

"That money isn't from my dad selling the mill, it's to upgrade it. Whatever the Sheriff told you, he was wrong."

Carl crumpled his mouth into an upturned smile. His forehead creased into a lined frown. He was stumped. What the hell?

The words carved into a locker door seemed to say it all: someone had scratched 'IDIOT' in large letters. Carl glanced at it, and lowered the Glock to his hip.

Aaron took this chance to open his clenched hand – containing the shotgun shell that had previously rolled under the lockers.

He rammed the shell into the breach, pumping the shotgun.

"Pineville isn't going to die..." Aaron said, suddenly drawing Carl's attention back to him. "You are, dumbass."

Staring back at him, Carl's glassy eyes – in Aaron's cross-hairs, just like the doe on that hunting trip with his dad, Derek. But, Aaron wasn't able to pull the trigger that time. Despite his father's commands for a kill shot - *"Go on, Aaron. Do it. Do it!"* - Aaron couldn't; he was unable to pull the trigger and finish what his father started. Disappointed in his son's lack of killer instinct, Derek aimed his rifle and took care of business. Well, so much for their manly bonding trip to the woods.

However, this time was different. Unlike the doe's innocence, Aaron could only see greed and evil in Carl's eyes. All bred out of money. The mill. His father.

Pumping the shotgun with a loud 'shunk', Aaron fired at Carl who was raising his Glock not quickly enough. The blast blew Carl back several feet, taking it full in the chest. A vest could have stopped the hit, but Carl, cowboy that he was, was no longer wearing it.

"Shit..." Carl's voice descended into gurgles as the holes ventilating his chest filled with blood.

Just as it was for Tremblay, it was curtains for Carl. The timid boy that was afraid to fire in the woods with his Dad, no longer existed.

LEE CHAMBERS

thirty nine

Staggering from the building, Aaron was three shades of red. Spurts of Tremblay, splatter from Carl and with scars of his own---all blending into a smorgasbord of mauve and burgundy. As a result, Aaron's shirt looked like a Jackson Pollack-inspired masterpiece; tentatively titled '*Dead Man Walking*'.

Amanda rushed from Carl's cruiser to Aaron's side, her face emblazoned with shock and pity. "Aaron, oh my God. Are you alright?"

"It's not all my blood," Aaron explained, still in a daze. The sun was peeking over the horizon. Finally, daybreak was coming. A sunrise washes away all sins. Makes everything seem clean again. Aaron was ready for a fresh start, a new lease on life.

"What happened? Where's, Carl?" Amanda continued with her questions, looking around Aaron, expecting Carl to walk outside, too. "Is he still in there?"

Aaron shook his head. She could immediately read the foreboding doom in his expression. "He didn't make it." Aaron's words hung in the air.

"Oh, no, Aaron, no, no, no..." Amanda's voice descended into wails and blubbering. She suddenly latched onto the closest warm body – Aaron's. Holding him tight, sobbing uncontrollably into his chest.

Aaron looked down, snapping out of his comatose state, and patted her tenderly on the back. An awkward moment, considering he dealt the fatal blow, not Tremblay. Not really the time to spill the beans that her knight in shining armor was not so clean after all. Unsure what else to do, he simply stood there and let her cry.

Both Tremblay and Carl were the masterminds of a devious plan to rip off what they suspected was soon to be a dead city. Dead. Aaron had seen plenty of that in the last 14 hours - even more carnage than his hunting trip. An innocent doe and now a bunch of dead bodies. People he knew - Steve and Principal Parker as innocent as the deer in the woods. He was still in shock. How could this all happen in Pineville?

In the orange tinge of the rising sun, red and white flashing lights entered the parking lot - a police cruiser chirped its siren as it led an ambulance onto the scene, followed by a procession of local cars. The EMTs quickly jumped out of the back of the ambulance, carrying their medical kits, and running towards Amanda and Aaron.

Within minutes, Amanda had a warm blanket wrapped around her shoulders and she was whisked into the ambulance. Similarly draped in a blanket, Aaron was brought in and sat on the bench opposite her.

Just before Aaron could get comfortable, a large man appeared in the doorway of the ambulance, a pad and pen in his outstretched hand. "I need to get your statement, son," said the cop, staring coolly at Aaron.

Aaron looked over at Amanda with trepidation. She was his responsibility now. Wasn't she? When a lady cries on your shoulder, you need to stay with her? Aaron wasn't sure, but Amanda smiled calmly and said, "It's okay, Aaron. I'll be fine."

She'll be fine. It was over. Aaron nodded and stepped out with the cop. He glanced back towards her, as the other EMT closed the ambulance's rear double-doors one by one, and then moved around to the driver's door. After another slam, an engine started and the ambulance pulled away. *Goodbye, Miss Becker.*

"Get me down from here!"

"Mikey!" Aaron exclaimed as a cluster of cops looked sky-wards. Mike was waving his shirt over his head, drawing their attention. "Thank God you are okay!"

Just to see a friendly face, Aaron couldn't help but smile.

forty

Aaron and Mike were sitting side by side in the back of a police cruiser, with the door slung open, waiting for the results of the room-by-room investigation at the school.

"I can't believe that Steve..." Mike shook his head, hardly able to bring himself to say the ugly words.

"I know, I know," Aaron said consolingly. "Mister Parker, too."

One of the cops wandered from the school, just as a limo bounced into the parking lot, skidding to a halt in front of the cop.

"Shit." Aaron knew exactly who had arrived. The whole town recognized that limo as Derek Stevens, the mill killer.

Right on cue, Derek hopped out, talked pensively to the cop, who pointed over in Aaron's direction. Aaron slid out of the cruiser and awaited the onslaught either of condemnation, discipline, concern, or all three.

"Oh my God, Aaron," Derek blurted out, seeing the red stains beneath the gray polyester blanket around Aaron's shoulders.

"It's okay, Dad, I'll be fine."

"Is he under arrest yet?" Derek turned to the cop, before flicking back to Aaron. "Don't say anything until I get you a lawyer."

"Under arrest? For what?" Aaron asked, perturbed.

Derek looked from Aaron to the cop, unsure of what was actually going on. Both faces, Aaron and the officer in charge, seemed equally blank.

"I don't understand. Tremblay said you and your friends... were involved."

"And you believed him?" Aaron choked. "Tremblay did it, Dad."

"What?"

"Tremblay and Carl stole your precious money, not me. And thanks a lot." Aaron pouted, surprising himself that he even had enough energy to care about his father's low opinion of him, as a potential bank robbery suspect. Had Aaron survived the night of the Pineville Heist for nothing? What started as a mad moment under the canoe, a split decision to take the money in the first place, led Aaron down a road to manhood. It wasn't pretty, it wasn't easy. But Aaron grew balls in the midnight hours. He found confidence to stand up for himself. He braved evil and came out on top.

The officer nodded, supporting Aaron's side of things. "It's true, Mister Stevens. The money's inside the school. If it wasn't for your son here, they would have gotten away with it."

"And if it wasn't for Amanda calling the cops, you wouldn't have me or the money, so screw you, Dad."

"Amanda?" The officer raised a quizzical eyebrow.

"Yeah, you know... Miss Becker." Aaron thumbed over his shoulder, pointing to where the ambulance was parked earlier. "My teacher."

"Miss Becker didn't call us down here. He did," the officer nodded to Mike--who, from the few hours spent on the rooftop, half the time spent shirtless and waving at cars was now slightly shaking. "You should be thanking him for flagging down a passing truck."

Puzzle pieces were scattering in front of Aaron, a jumble in his subconscious. He thought he had it figured out. All the pieces seemed to fit, but now one giant part of the puzzle was missing...

178

Amanda. Where was she now? With her bandaged up foot, she had discharged herself from the hospital. A case of shock, go home, get some rest.

Yet, rest was the last thing on Amanda's mind as she stepped into the back of a waiting taxi cab.

It was a short drive from the hospital. The sun was rising through the trees of the forest. A low mist was starting to burn off, leaving a tranquil woodland scene, with dew on the bluebells and glistening on the bark of the towering redwoods.

The cabbie wasn't confident that he'd driven Amanda to where she wanted to be. "Are you sure about this? There's nothing out here."

Amanda was sure. "I'll just be a few minutes. Wait here."

She stepped out of the cab and wandered down a muddy sidetrack. In her pocket, her cellphone; Amanda flipped the lid, revealing that it was actually a portable GPS unit. Same make and model as the GPS unit that one of the hapless bank robbers, Gordie, had punched coordinates into. In fact, it was the exact same GPS unit.

The screen illuminated as Amanda pressed a button; a pre-entered location popped up on the screen with a subdued beep. Not too far from where she was standing.

Quite out of place in the woods, Amanda's work shoes were getting dirty. No matter, she could buy plenty more. Her wounded foot was hurting now but nothing that a few weeks in Aruba couldn't fix. Hell, a few years in Aruba.

The beep was getting louder and more frequent. She was honing in on her destination. Just behind this next clump of trees. Under some brush, instead of an 'X', a wooden plank marked the spot.

Amanda tossed the GPS device on the ground and pre-pared to get dirtier. She clawed her manicured nails beneath the plank and dragged it from the hole. Dusting her hands on her skirt, she leaned over the edge – at the bottom of the ditch, Jake, Gordie and Steve's corpses.

"Oh Jesus, Carl…"

The smell hit Amanda's nostrils and she stepped back repulsed, then leaned in for a second look – beneath the pile of bodies, she saw a welcome sight. The green backpack, bulging with stolen cash.

Despite her disgust, Amanda wasn't about to let a couple of stiffs get in the way of her and all that money. She'd come too far to bail now.

Screwing up her face, Amanda reached her arm down, over the top of Gordie, and grabbed the protruding strap of the backpack. It was heavy and wedged under Gordie's shoulder. Amanda leaned in closer for better leverage, straining and breaking a small sweat.

Now her face was a mere inch or two from Gordie's white, rolled-back eyeballs. And the pack of cigarettes, wedged in his top pocket. Her brand, as it so happened.

Then with a big tug, the backpack came loose and Amanda brought it out of the hole. Taking a deep breath, she hurled the bag to the ground, and she paused for a split second. Made up her mind. "Screw it."

Amanda knelt back down and stuck her arm back into the hole. Her hand re-emerged with Gordie's pack of cigarettes. A girl's gotta do, what a girl's gotta do.

Flipping open the pack, Amanda put a cigarette into her mouth. Holding the filter between her teeth, she patted her skirt pockets. No lighter.

With a grimace, Amanda leaned over the edge of the hole. It would be worth it, she thought.

And she was right. Walking along, with the backpack hanging from her shoulders, and the lit cigarette burning from her happy lips. Not too shabby, Miss Becker.

The trail ended here and she was free and clear. There was nothing to tie her to the crimes of four scheming criminals. She would play out the rest of the semester as the dust settled and then quietly walk away from the high school and Pineville for good. With Carl no longer in the picture, Amanda imagined dropping some dough on a small and swanky ocean view apartment in Marina del Rey. Take in some LA sunshine. A devious smile shone across her face.

Yet, her smile quickly turned into a displeased scowl. The taxi was gone, leaving a tell-tale set of tire tracks in the mud.

"Son of a…"

"Bitch," Aaron finished her thought, whilst stating his own.

Amanda whirled around to see Aaron with several officers who he'd led down to the wooded area.

Her mouth curved into a perfect 'o' and the cigarette – that she struggled so hard for – tumbled from her lips, extinguishing with a fizz in a brown puddle at her feet.

"I have to hand it to you, Miss Becker. It turns out you really are quite the actress after all," Aaron said to the stunned woman; now a virtual stranger. The Miss Becker that Aaron thought he knew had retracted turtle-style into the shell of this body, leaving only a criminal caught red-handed. "I reckon you deserve an Academy frickin' Award, for sure."

"What?" she said sheepishly, feeling the police officers' eyes crawling all over her.

The officer in charge took a large step towards Amanda, and she immediately recoiled a step backwards. Her eyes were frightened and dancing around the faces surrounding her. "We found this on Carl," the officer announced, producing an envelope - with two plane tickets inside. "Two tickets to Aruba; in Carl's and your names. Planning a little trip, were we?"

Amanda went on the defensive: "So what? It's no secret we were dating. How could you…"

Aaron quickly interrupted her argument, "They were one way, Miss Becker! It's pretty hard to put a play on Monday night when you were planning on sipping margaritas with Carl on a beach, don't you think?"

In his other hand, the officer revealed a pair of shiny handcuffs. Amanda stepped back again, but this time bumped into another officer behind her. She let out a tiny yelp. The officer unzipped the backpack and nodded to his superior. "Pineville bank bags," he called out.

Her face dropped. "I'm sorry, Aaron," Amanda said, staring down at the murky puddle, with the cigarette slowly circling the water.

"And you didn't even call for help? You just sat in that car thinking of ways to spend the money… knowing I wasn't ever going to come out of that school alive."

"I'm sorry!"

"Tremblay said they'd stashed the rest of the money near the campsite. So, I knew it was the only way to be sure about you, by returning to the woods, to see if you were 'in' on it," said Aaron, with a shake of his head. "Honestly, I could've expected this much of Tremblay, maybe even Carl, but not you, Amanda. How could *you*? I trusted you. Saved your life…"

"I'm so, so sorry Aaron."

"Yeah… me too," Aaron shook his head and looked away. He couldn't look at her anymore. "Me too."

Aaron watched the cops slap on the metal cuffs and start pushing Amanda away, leaving the backpack on the ground. She watched it reluctantly disappear from her. Mascara staining her cheeks. Crying partly for the money, partly for Carl, but mostly for herself. Confusion about the mill setting

182

all these nasty chain of events in motion. Her dreams and plans shattered by greed. Now all Amanda's confidence and strength was with Aaron. He assumed a new role and stood tall. Taller than he ever had before.

The officer in charge glanced at Aaron, who was looking solemn, broken and really damn tired. "So, what about you, kid?"

"The show must go on."

forty one

RRRRIIIIIIIINNNNNNNNNGGGGG.

The bell signaled the end of class. Within seconds, the janitor disappeared back inside the maintenance room and the freshly-mopped hallways of Pineville High School were filled shoulder-to-shoulder with adolescent students.

They wandered past the library – still closed for cleaning and asbestos removal – of which there was none – and the empty Principal's office.

Two weeks had passed them by. The school had closed down. Time needed to clean up some of the mess. Get over the devastation and loss. Consider it an early holiday for the 234 students. But time stands still for no one except the dead. The spirit of Pineville can't be stopped and another night of carnage was about to ensue – that being the fake stage deaths in Hamlet.

Amongst the throng of kids, Aaron and Mike emerged from English class. The substitute teacher, a bookish woman, gathered up her belongings and her '#1 Teacher' coffee mug and ventured off to the staff room in search of a re-fill.

As Aaron made his way to his locker, a few students slapped him on the back, giving him thumbs-up gestures and tossing out cordial comments like "Way to go," "Hey, Aaron," "Break a leg tonight, man."

Despite feeling ready and rehearsed, having spent more time treading the boards of the school stage than many of the other actors, particularly after his impromptu sword-fighting with the former Sheriff; these well-wishers only added to the tension creeping up Aaron's spine and the twisting pit in his stomach since his half-eaten bowl of Cheerios that morning.

Nevertheless, Aaron smiled and reciprocated several high-fives before opening his locker. He pulled his Hamlet book off the top shelf and stared at the mud and water stains spread across it. The corners damaged and worn. He rubbed his hand across the cover. A sly smile crept across his face. He reached further into the locker and fumbled around to grab his frilly costume.

There was a newspaper clipping, taped haphazardly to the inside of the locker door: "Town Pays Tribute To Hero Student At Parker Memorial." On the same clipping, a headline to a missing article: "Stevens Completes Mill Purchase: Announces Expansion."

"Is he coming?"

Aaron turned abruptly, slamming the locker door, and looked into the dazzling green eyes of the pretty girl from his English class, Marissa. Shrugging nonchalantly, Aaron tucked the copy of Hamlet and his costume under his arm, and strolled down the corridor beside Marissa.

"Well, good luck tonight anyway."

"Thanks," Aaron said a little shocked she was actually talking to him. It was really a first. The object of his affections since her family moved to Pineville from the big city of Thunder Bay at the start of the semester, Marissa was quickly drawn into the 'punish all things Stevens' fan club. He had all but given up on her. Things can really change on a dime or in his case millions. This could be good.

"What are you doing after?" Marissa asked, stroking the back of her arm, looking shyly in the opposite direction. She was pretty. Very pretty and her direct stare was intoxicating.

"Uh... nothing." Aaron shrugged again. He felt his heart actually skip a beat.

"Cool. Maybe we could do something?" Marissa said with a smile, which Aaron could feel shine right through him. This was going better than he could've hoped.

He opened the door for her, and carried her smile on his face for the rest of the day, and the rest of the night. Opening night.

forty two

Things looked very different from the last time Aaron was on the same stage. Beside him, Mike was dressed for the part of Horatio, in an equally frilly outfit as Aaron was wearing.

Pete, dressed up nicely as he could in Goth attire looked relieved to be sitting in the front row. With trusty Charlotte by his side, looking bored out of her mind, silence fell over the packed house. All eyes forward, watching the action unfold. No one truly knew what evil took place on this very stage. But, Aaron did and he channeled it all into giving the best performance he could.

Aaron's Hamlet was bent down on one knee, looking up at Horatio.

"Oh, I die, Horatio. The potent poison quite o'er-crows my spirit," Aaron – in character – quivered for a second. *"I cannot live to hear the news from England, but I do prophesy the election lights. On Fortinbras, he has my dying voice, so tell him, with the occurrents, more and less, which have solicited. The rest is silence..."*

With that, Aaron keeled over on the stage - "dead."

Mike continued the play's finale, turning to another boy from their English class. *"Now cracks a noble heart. Good night, sweet prince..."*

The curtain began to lower in front of Aaron's half-closed eyes. As the audience eclipsed in front of him, he scanned the faces – searching, searching, searching, but not finding the one that he sought. Suddenly, he heard the thunderous applause and the curtain had touched down, blocking his view.

Aaron looked to Mike, who reached out a hand, lifting him to his feet. "I'm sure he tried to make it," Mike said, reading his friend's mind. They shuffled to their positions with the other actors and waited for the curtain call.

The clapping continued as the fabric rose, revealing the players again to the crowd. Aaron nodded to the applause and cheers of the audience; however, his scanning eyes settled on a single empty chair, his father's chair.

Suddenly above the steady clap, Aaron perceived another pair of hands, vigorous and extra loud. There at the side of stage right stood Derek Stevens and beaming with great pride, as he started a standing ovation.

Aaron couldn't contain the grin spreading across his face. He savoured the moment, one unforgettable harmonious sound to be forever treasured.

The rest is silence.

about the author

Born and raised in Sault Ste. Marie in Northern Ontario,
Canada, Lee Chambers is an award-winning writer and
director. After ten years in the UK and Los Angeles, he is back
in Canada making films, along with his duties teaching
screenwriting and film production.

www.leechambers.com

15181916R00103

Made in the USA
Charleston, SC
21 October 2012